The Lady and the Luddite

# The Lady and the Luddite

## Linden Salter

ROBERT HALE · LONDON

ISBN 0 7090 6609 0

Robert Hale Limited
Clerkenwell House
Clerkenwell Green
London EC1R 0HT

2 4 6 8 10 9 7 5 3 1

08130596

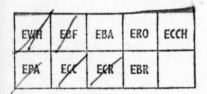

| EWH | EBF | EBA | ERO | ECCH |
|-----|-----|-----|-----|------|
| EPA | ECC | ECR | EBR |      |

Typeset by
Derek Doyle & Associates, Liverpool.
Printed in Great Britain by
St Edmundsbury Press, Bury St Edmunds, Suffolk.
Bound by WBC Book Manufacturers Limited, Bridgend.

*To Brian, my favourite Yorkshireman*

# Acknowledgements

This book owes the greatest debt to Charlotte Brontë. Rather than create my own fictional background to the story of the Luddites, I have used one that she created in her neglected novel *Shirley*: the setting, many of the characters, and some of the plot and language are hers, although this is not merely a rewriting of her work. Charlotte Brontë's Shirley knew nothing of Tom Mellor: I hope that Brontë admirers will forgive the liberties I have taken.

I am also very grateful to Miyoko and Richard Britton, to Cleckheaton Public Library in West Yorkshire, to all those who read and commented on drafts, and to the Northern Territory Department of Arts and Museums for a grant which helped in the final stages of editing. I have used a number of resources, many of which are listed at the end: the responsibility for any errors that appear is mine.

# PART I

The dog was clearly mad. The warning cries behind me would have told me, even if I had not seen the foam at its muzzle, its staggering gait, and the shake of its head vainly trying to rid itself of its agony.

'Run!' I heard a shout from Sir Philip, to whom I was betrothed. 'Shirley, run away!'

But I could not. Between me and safety was the length of the coach and its horses. We had stopped at the smithy as one of the horses had cast a shoe. Sir Philip and the coachman were inside with the smith attending to it, and I had stepped out on the road side of the coach to walk a little way through the village.

Then the mad dog appeared, sweeping the village clear of people. It saw me and dragged itself towards me, panting and whining. Perhaps its mind still told it that I was a person, a master, someone who could help it. But I knew that if I turned and fled, it would attack me.

I had never seen anyone die of hydrophobia, but I had read enough to know what would happen. Screaming insanely, a terror to all around me so that only relief would greet my inevitable end – yes, I was afraid.

I prayed that the dog still had the remnants of its training and would obey the word of command. I mustered all my authority. 'Sit!' I said sternly. Thank God! I thought, as it obeyed clumsily, its back legs buckling. If I moved slowly and cautiously, perhaps I could reach safety inside the coach. It was a closed carriage with a door that must be opened, and steps that must be climbed.

I reached backwards to the handle. The dog snarled: a terrible, hopeless snarl that warned me to move no more. It staggered to its feet and came towards me step by dragging step. 'Sit!' I ordered again: it did not obey, but it stopped moving, torn between its training and its insanity.

Behind me the voices had quietened to a panicking whisper of confusion, as one voice suggested moving the carriage out of the way, another prohibited it for fear of making the dog attack, a third – Sir Philip – whispering only, 'But we must do something!'

Then another voice, one I'd never heard before: a man with a broad Yorkshire accent. 'Do you keep a gun?'

'There's one in the carriage by the door, but it's not loaded,' came the coachman's voice.

'That's good for nowt!' said the man. 'Where's the powder and shot?'

'Give it to him,' said Sir Philip to the coachman. 'You can shoot, my man?'

'Aye, I can shoot.'

How strange! My memory holds this whole conversation from fifty years ago, yet at the time my entire being seemed concentrated on holding the dog still by the force of my gaze alone.

Behind me I heard the sound of someone getting into the carriage, taking the pistol, loading it: then his voice, calm, but muffled through the glass of the coach window. 'Lady, can you hold the dog steady while I open the door? If you can't, say now and I'll shoot through the glass – but happen that'll spoil the shot.'

'I can hold it,' I said, strangely assured of my power over the dog's madness. Out of the corner of my eye I could see the door opening unobtrusively. The dog whined but did not move.

'This'll make a great loud noise right by your ear, lady.' His voice seemed competent and confident, and helped me to control my fear. 'When it does, jump into the coach as fast as you can. Ready?'

'Yes.'

There was a noise – but not a deafening one. The gun had misfired!

The dog snarled and leapt at me; a powerful arm went round my waist and hauled me backwards into the coach. But the dog was on me: it grabbed my foot. I kicked out desperately trying to shake the boot off, but it wouldn't come, and the dog was chewing viciously into the leather.

I fell on to the floor of the coach, still kicking, as the man dropped me. He dived over me towards the dog. With one hand he grabbed the dog by the neck; with the other he smashed the pistol straight down on its head.

Just once: it was all that was needed. The dog dropped, instantly dead from the mighty blow to its brain.

There was a babble of voices and a rush of hands carrying me to a seat in the smithy. I began to untie my boot, chewed and torn. I said nothing, could feel nothing for a moment: not until I knew.

'I say, that was the bravest thing I've ever seen,' Sir Philip said. The man who had saved me was dusting himself down as he walked slowly into the smithy; from his rough clothes and coarse hands he was clearly a working man. 'I can't thank you enough, my man,' Sir Philip continued. 'You rescued Miss Keeldar from an atrocious fate.'

'Happen I did, happen I didn't,' said the man. 'Were you bitten?' he asked me.

I took my boot off. It had protected me from the dog's bite –

but not entirely. There on my leg was a tear of flesh, bleeding slowly. Not a big wound. But, I feared, big enough.

'And you?' I asked.

He looked down at his left arm. It too was bleeding. We stared at each other: he a working man, I a gentlewoman, joined in a democracy of terror that for a moment excluded everyone, everything else in the world.

It is as if there is a picture of him at that moment in my mind, like one of those new-fangled photographs that everyone has on their walls nowadays. But a photograph could show only his appearance: his determined face with the lines from laughter still drawn there though he was far from laughing then, the big muscular body that might writhe with madness and agony in the next months, the coarse clothes and clogs that marked the great distance there was between us in the world's estimation despite our union at that moment. A photograph could not show what I saw most clearly then: the qualities that had made him risk a fearful death to save a stranger, and could find room, in the midst of his own horror, to think of me in mine.

'Quick, water!' I heard the coachman shout. 'Wash the wounds. Try to get the poison out before it spreads.'

Water splashed over my ankle and the man's arm, and hands washed and scrubbed at our wounds.

'I've heard it said,' the smith said uncertainly, 'that cauterization will cure a dog bite, if it's done fast enough.'

'You mean – burn the wound?' said Sir Philip. 'Oh – but – Miss Keeldar couldn't stand the pain.'

'Miss Keeldar will certainly stand the pain if it means she doesn't die in screaming agony,' I said briefly.

The smith held up two irons, hot from the forge. One for me: one for the man. He took them both, then gave one to me. Even the cooler end of the iron was so hot that it took all my resolution to grasp it. Could I bear the red heat on my wound?

'I can take it if you can,' said the man, daring me to draw back. Without a word, I put the red hot iron on my wound. A scream forced its way to my lips, and my coward hand betrayed me and pulled the iron away.

Then I looked at the man. His hand hadn't flinched. He grinned at me, his white teeth clenched as the iron scorched his skin. His glittering blue eyes held mine, giving me courage to do what I must. Yes, I could and I would do it, I knew as I applied the iron again. The pain seemed to last for ever, but it must have been only a few seconds before I heard Sir Philip say, 'That's enough.'

'Aye, that's enough,' said the man. He put down the iron, nodded to me, and walked out of the smithy.

Sir Philip made to follow him, but I held out my hand to stop him. I knew how the man felt. He wanted no one to talk to him, no meaningless chatter, no thanks or praise. He was faced, as I was, with a fearful prospect. Perhaps our pain had paid the price and averted that terrible death – but perhaps it hadn't.

I was a month short of my twenty-first birthday. Twenty-one! For years I had looked forward to December the nineteenth, 1811, as the day when I would at last be free of the strong, silken rope that bound me to the will of my guardian.

Reader, please don't think of Mr Sympson as some wicked uncle out of a melodrama. He would no more have cheated me out of my fortune than he would have laughed in church. He was, in a word, respectable. He had respectably taken me into his home near Bath when I was left an orphan. He had respectably raised me with his respectable daughters. He had respectably tended my inheritance so that it was now a more than respectable sum. His respectable wife had ensured that I met respectable suitors, and there was respectable rejoicing when I accepted Sir Philip Nunnely's offer of marriage.

In the whole of my life there were only three people who did not reek of respectability, only three with whom I could have a conversation that might suggest that there was something more important.

Mrs Pryor had the appearance of complete respectability, or she would not have been taken on to be governess to me and my girl cousins. But, when the day was over, and she and I would converse in the easy way of old friends with nothing else to do, there was a hint that her respectability was a refuge from something else. Perhaps I had read too many novels, but I could fancy that Mrs Pryor had a Past.

My young cousin Henry had an intellect of formidable power in a body left lame from a childhood illness. Though only fifteen, he had a better-informed mind than any of the young men who sought my looks and my fortune in marriage. The mind was his own: much of the information came from his tutor, the third person with whom I could talk.

I would listen, rapt, to Louis Gerard's transmission of ideas from the world outside. He could have banished me from his lessons with Henry, but he turned a blind eye. It was no wonder that for many years I had nourished what I thought was a passion for him. He seemed to carry a world of knowledge in his head, and he shared it with me generously. He understood my feelings, and neither laughed at me nor took advantage of my infatuation. When, inevitably, I outgrew my feelings for him (along with my spots and puppy fat), he bore no resentment, and wished me well when he learned of my engagement to another man.

I wished I felt one tenth of the passion for Sir Philip that I'd once had for Mr Gerard. But I identified that passion with schoolgirl infatuation, and thought that, in the real world of husbands and wives, of gentlemen and ladies, passion had no part.

I liked Sir Philip well enough. He was handsome in a delicate way: a slight frame and sandy hair were accompanied by a pleasant smile showing even white teeth. Though he had none of Mr Gerard's learning or intellect, he was not stupid. His most unfortunate feature was his taste for writing poems, which he would insist on reading to me, especially those which he had written in my honour. Unluckily for him, the few words that rhyme with Shirley include *curly*, *girly* and *burly*, none of which apply to me with any degree of truth.

I must state that I did not accept him for his rank and fortune. I had no interest in his title, though my uncle and aunt were delighted that I should marry a baronet. I had more than enough fortune of my own to want his: one thousand pounds a year would be mine when I turned twenty-one. I accepted his offer because I thought it would bring my freedom. As Sir Philip's betrothed, I could accept his mother's invitation to stay with them in the West Riding, away from Bath and the Sympsons, and just a few miles from my own, longed-for house of Fieldhead.

Mr Sympson could never understand my longing to get back to the home of my childhood. To him it was just a rambling sixteenth-century house, gloomy with its oak panelling and chimneys that whistled when the wind blew. He could not like its small windows nor the thick walls that kept out the Yorkshire cold. I had not seen it since my parents died. To me, Fieldhead represented both home – the home of my childhood – and freedom, the freedom to do what I wanted in my own property.

Sir Philip wanted me to go north with him as his wife, of course; but I had persuaded him that it was better for me to marry him when I came of age and could dispose of my fortune as I pleased, rather than as my uncle desired. Indeed, it was not hard for me to persuade Sir Philip to do anything –

persuadability was one of his charms for a young woman who wanted her own way. So, with Mrs Pryor to ensure my respectability, and his mother to ensure his, I had been living in Nunnely Hall for some months.

I judged that Lady Nunnely must once have been a beauty. I could see the remains in her face, her son had inherited her looks, and there was no other possible reason why Sir Philip's father would have married her. She was devoted to her son, admired his poems, and had no other interest save fashion and the iniquities of her servants: an unjustified charge, since the servants ran Nunnely Hall with no help from her. I would not have an interfering mother-in-law when I became mistress of the Hall, so I was not disposed to complain.

She already showed every willingness to place the running of the household on my shoulders, though I was merely Sir Philip's betrothed. I avoided the responsibility by saying that I needed to devote myself to bringing my own house into order.

That was not merely an excuse. Bad tenants followed by years of emptiness had let the elements eat into the walls of Fieldhead – and Yorkshire elements are some of the more voracious, and need to be kept at bay with a firm hand. Sir Philip and I had driven over every week of that warm autumn after a cold summer to watch the progress, and every visit made it seem more like a home to be lived in.

It was on our way back from one visit that we had our encounter with the mad dog. And that changed everything.


Dr Kerr finished rebandaging my wound, and nodded to himself.

'I've not heard of cauterizing a dog bite, but it can't do any harm, and may have done some good,' he said approvingly.

'Do you think that I'll catch the infection now?' I asked.

'Ah, tsh, tsh. It's not for a young girl like you to be worrying about rabies,' he said heartily. 'Plenty of good food, fresh air and exercise, that's my advice.'

I was in no mood for his heartiness. 'Dr Kerr, with my own hand I held a red hot iron against that bite. I am brave enough to take whatever information you have to give me. I have decisions to make that will be affected by what you tell me, so I must have the truth.'

I'd seen that look before: the look that men give when they realize that they are talking not just to a pretty young woman but to a rational human being.

'Well, Miss Keeldar, the truth is that I don't know. It was only a small bite, and you dealt with it promptly.'

'So my chances are good?'

'Yes, yes, yes,' he said with relief that was obviously sincere.

'Exactly what chances? If this were a horse-race, what odds would you give?'

He seemed shocked at my sporting comparison, but then nodded again. 'At the moment? I'd say about evens. If there is no sign of infection after three months, then much better than that: say ten to one. The earliest the infection could take hold is about ten days. If it does, there will be irritability and depression, fever, nausea, and a sore throat. But I sincerely believe that you will probably escape.'

'How long will it be before I can be completely certain of that?'

'Well – it was a small bite, and though that means you're less likely to be infected, it also means that it will be a good deal longer before we can be completely certain that you're safe: six months, or even a year.'

'There was a man who was bitten at the same time – bitten much worse than I. What are his chances?'

'If he is free of infection after three months, then you will certainly be safe. If not – well, you shouldn't despair: his bite was worse than yours. If I were you, I should watch that man very closely.'

I had not thought much on religion before, accepting God in much the same way as I accepted the wallpaper – something there in the background, but nothing that I took much notice of. What young woman with good looks and fortune ever does think much of serious things? But the imminence of death is a great evangelist. I prayed harder and more sincerely than I had ever done in my life, and gained a little comfort.

I gained some comfort too from Mrs Pryor. I told her what had happened, and what I could expect. She sympathized like a sensible woman, not so profusely as to upset me further, but enough. Then she wisely set me to practising my music: it kept my thoughts occupied. I could hardly keep playing the piano for the next three months, but at least I could get through that evening.

Or so I thought until Sir Philip joined us. He held my hand speechlessly, his eyes blinking back the tears, and I knew that he loved me, and I loved him at that moment more than I had ever done before. But then he fumbled in his coat and produced a sheet of paper. 'I have written you a poem, my love,' he said, and started to recite it:

> '*My dear, my sweet, my young and lovely Shirley.*
> *My wife to be – the mother of my babies.*
> *How sad I am that you may die so early.*
> *How bad the dog that bit you with the rabies.*'

'Sir Philip—' I began, but he went on, leaving me with the thought that if irritability, depression and nausea were early symptoms, then the infection had taken hold already.

*'How scared I was when you were by the carriage*
*And th' wicked dog was chewing at your shoe.*
*Oh, darling, let us hasten on our marriage*
*So I may, as your husband, care for you.'*

'Sir Philip!' I said again, and this time would not let him continue, for I knew then that, of all the people in the world, he was the last that I would want to care for me if I were to sicken and die. 'We cannot be married!' I blurted out.

He recoiled, his face white. 'But why not?'

How could I tell him that I would not marry him because of his bad verse? 'I would not have you marry a madwoman, my dear,' I said gently.

'I don't care! I want to marry you. For better, or for worse. I love you.'

'It's because you love me that I could not bear to have you watch me die in agonized insanity. Don't you see that? It would just make it worse for me.'

He turned away, reached into his pocket for a handkerchief and blew his nose. 'Yes, my darling, I do see that,' he said, a crack in his voice. 'I cannot press you further.'

My affection for this kind, unselfish man came back, and I held out some hope for him. 'The doctor says that, if the infection has not appeared within the year, I shall be safe. If God is good, it is only a postponement.'

'A year? It's too long.'

'We've been engaged nearly a year already; we can manage another, if it means that we can be free of this dread.'

'Oh, my love!' He turned back to me, and for the first time ever, he took me in his arms and kissed me on the lips. 'If you can be so brave, so can I.'

I wished I could feel for him the passion that he so clearly felt for me. But his embrace, his kiss did not stir me. I felt only affection and pity for him. Yes, I could marry him in a year. If only I could wean him away from poetry. . . .

The smithy in Briarfield had not changed overnight: I had. When, just the day before, I had alighted from the carriage to take a stroll through the village, it had not struck me as a gloomy place, but now I saw it as a condemned man might see the gallows. I approached the smith, who looked at me with fascinated pity: and I knew at that point that I must try to keep my condition secret, for I couldn't bear such looks from strangers.

I came to business. 'The man who saved me. I should like to find him.'

'I'm right sorry, Miss Keeldar, I can't help you.'

'You may understand my reasons. I wish to express my gratitude. And, if the worst should happen, I wish to make sure that his family is looked after.'

He turned back to the forge, and hammered out a ploughshare desultorily. 'He were a stranger to me,' he said after a while. 'I can't tell you his name.'

There was something about his voice, his stance, that told me he was lying. 'Will you look me in the eye and tell me that you don't know anything about this man?' I asked.

He said nothing.

'Can't you see that I want nothing but good for him?' I pleaded. 'I may die a horrible death in the near future, as may he. Nothing will stop his wife and children's grief at losing such a strong, brave man, one who sacrificed his life for another. But if I know that at least they will not suffer financially, it would ease my dying, and it might ease his.'

'He has no wife, no children,' the smith muttered reluctantly after a moment. 'You've no need to fash yourself with them.'

'You do know him, then?'

'Aye. But I'll say nowt else about him.'

'Why not, pray?'

Silence. I would get no more out of him.

*Why?*

Since you have this testimony in your hand, reader, you will know that I did not die of hydrophobia fifty years ago at the age of twenty-one, and I shall not try your patience with more than a brief account of what I went through then. Have you ever had a nagging tooth? You know how sometimes it fills the whole of your mind, and at other times you hardly notice it, and can appear to the world as if nothing were amiss? But it is always there.

So it was with my fear. If I do not mention it in my narrative of the events that happened during that period, do not imagine it was absent. At some times it was worse than others; when I fell sick with a fever and sore throat, Mrs Pryor had to work very hard to convince me that the accompanying running nose and sneezes were far more likely to be the symptoms of a good Yorkshire cold than of anything more sinister.

At least I could keep myself busy. I had to persuade all those who knew about my danger to keep quiet, for I could not bear fascinated, pitying looks. I had to fob my guardian off with an excuse as to why I was not yet marrying Sir Philip. I had to make my will; Mr Pearson, once my father's lawyer, was eager to be mine, and he agreed to bring it to me to sign on the day I came of age. Most of all, I had to make sure that Fieldhead was in order. For I decided that, if I were alive and healthy when I came of age, I would move there. No Mr Sympson, no Sir Philip, could stop me. With Mrs Pryor as my companion, I would be free and independent for the rest of my life, however long that would be.

Whenever I was out, I tried to catch sight of the man who had

21

risked his life for me. Though I was reassured that he would leave no family to starve if he died, I would have been even more reassured to know that he hadn't died at all. But I never saw him. In my pessimistic moments I thought he was dead already. In my melodramatic moments, prompted by the smith's secrecy about him, I thought he was in hiding for some fearful crime. In my balanced moments I thought he'd left the area.

My twenty-first birthday came, and I woke that morning almost to happiness. I had arrived, in sound mind and health, at my freedom!

Sir Philip greeted me with a very pretty pair of pearl earrings, and Mrs Pryor gave me a scarf of softest Yorkshire wool which she had knitted. A parcel from the Sympsons produced a beautiful cashmere shawl from my uncle, and a reticule, silk handkerchiefs and gloves from his wife and daughters, all embroidered with that skill in which they had always far exceeded me. Cousin Henry showed the taste that you would expect from a scholarly fifteen-year-old boy: better in books than in jewellery. I donated the ugly gold bracelet he sent me to the parish poor box, but *Sense and Sensibility*, by an unknown author, provided me with hours of welcome escape from my fears. Racine's tragedies from Mr Gerard would provide escape of a different sort, as I picked my way through the original, lyrical French. Mr Pearson arrived soon after breakfast, bearing the best present of all: my will, the first document I could sign in my own right as an adult.

Then, at last, the journey to Fieldhead: to my home. To *my* home, *my* property, with no one to say what I could and could not do with it. Reader, you will think me worldly, and so I was, that day.

Sir Philip kissed me tenderly as I was leaving. 'I had thought this day to make you my bride,' he said. I wished I could love him more; the best I could do was to put on a sorrowful demeanour, and hide the joy of freedom that was bursting within me.

Mr Pearson drove me and Mrs Pryor in his coach. A warm fire burned in the huge open grate as we arrived, scenting the house with pine cones; the servants I had hired earlier were lined up in their best to welcome me. Mrs Gill, the housekeeper, was proud to show me round my own house, keen to point out the cleaning and polishing that had taken place under her command, eager to show me into my own bedroom, where my clothes and treasures were neatly bestowed.

I wanted to hug the house to myself: I loved every gloomy oak panel, every wall crooked with age, every tiny window. It was *mine!* So was the neat garden, with walls that kept out the Yorkshire wind but allowed the midwinter sun to warm away the frost. So were the fields, with thick-fleeced sheep grazing peacefully and profitably. And so, I discovered, was Hollows Mill.

'Yes, Miss Keeldar,' said Mr Pearson as he showed me round my estate. 'You own the land and the mill itself. Your father built it twenty years ago. The rent provides half your income.'

So I was a mill-owner, was I? I didn't feel like a mill-owner: not a hard-faced man with an eye for nothing more than *t'brass*. In the valley where the mill stood I could see activity: people bustling around, a wagon leaving loaded with bales.

'It's mine, is it? Then I presume I may walk round my own property?'

'Of course,' said Mr Pearson. 'Your tenant is a clothier named Robert Moore: he is usually to be found there at this time of day. Or at any time, come to think of it; he works himself at least as hard as he works his men and machines.'

The mill was four storeys high, a long, narrow building with great windows to let in the midwinter light and save on lamps.

It was sited next to the river which drove the huge mill-wheel that powered every machine within its walls. We were still some distance but we could hear the sound of the machines, each with its own rhythm. Behind us, we could still hear the random noises of nature: the bleating of the sheep, the whistling of the wind. Ahead of us was the pounding, steady, regular thump and crash of the machines.

We walked through the mighty iron gates, and were shown into the counting-house attached to the mill. The small, carpet-less room contained only a few plain chairs, a cupboard, a solid desk and an old farmhouse table, with nothing but plans and diagrams to decorate its walls.

Its only inhabitant stood up as we arrived. He was a tall, dark man, perhaps thirty. His finely chiselled features had a conti-nental look that reminded me of Louis Gerard; I discovered later that his mother was from Brussels, and that he'd lived only a few years in Yorkshire, where his father was born. His clothes distinguished him from his workmen; plain though they were, they bore the mark of a gentleman of taste, and fitted him well enough to reveal the strength of the body they covered. And the jaw, the eyes, the mouth all told of his determination and power.

Mr Pearson performed the introductions. Mr Robert Moore did not quite conceal his irritation at the interruption, but his words were polite enough as he offered to take us for a tour of the mill. I was, after all, the owner.

I had thought the noise in the counting-house bad enough: but at least we could hear each other if our voices were raised. In the mill itself even this was impossible: all communication was carried out by signs. I did not then understand the processes by which a greasy fleece was turned into fine cloth, though I resolved that day that I would understand it before long (Racine could wait). I write now with my later under-standing of what was going on in the mill: all I saw then was the machines, and the people who served them.

Yes, it was people who served the machines, not the other way round. Men with bright scarlet skins from the dye vats; women reaching over the spinning mules tending the bobbins; and little children under the machines to tie the yarns where they broke, crouching amid the fluff that the machines let fall in a powder like dusty snow.

The smell was everywhere. Grease from the fleeces, oil from the machines, dust from the yarns, all mixed with the sweat of two hundred hard-working people who could not afford to spend much time in bathing and laundry. Not the coal and soot that's the smell of factories these days, for this was powered by the water-mill, not a steam-engine.

And such power! It was hard to believe that so much came from the river flowing peacefully beside the building, but it did. The shafts from the huge mill-wheel, spinning so fast you could hardly see them move, carrying the power to the carding-machine with its millions of tiny teeth, pulling the tangled woollen fleece into soft, uniform lengths, ready to go to the hundreds of bobbins on the mules, all moving identically, each one spinning far more yarn, far more evenly, than any woman with a spinning wheel. On a different floor, rows of men worked on their looms, each weaving as fast as he could to keep pace with the spun thread that kept pouring at them from the mules.

Then rough woven cloth was taken down to be finished on the ground floor, where there seemed to be a deafening silence after the cacophony of the machinery upstairs. Men fulled the cloth to shrink it and make it denser, then stretched it out on tenterhooks to dry. Other men dragged rows of teazels through the cloth to raise the nap, and from there it went to the cropping boards. Cloth piled up in front of the croppers, for there was far more work than they could do.

The croppers were huge men, with muscles rippling in their arms as they wielded the cropping-shears, four foot long; they all had calluses on their wrists from their years of doing so. Yet these mighty men handled the heavy shears with the delicacy I would use to cut a piece of embroidery silk. They had to cut off the rough nap that the teazels had raised to make the finished cloth smooth and fit for a dandy's opera cloak or a débutante's pelisse. Their strength and skill governed the ultimate price of the work of the dyers, carders, spinners and weavers – yes, and of Mr Moore, and his foremen and clerks too. They had to crop the cloth fine and smooth; but one slip of the shears would cut into the cloth itself, and lower its value like a flaw in a diamond.

Reader, on that fact depended most of the events in the narrative to come. I did not understand that at the time, of course; but even then I could see that they were different from the other workers. They did not greet Mr Moore with a scared look and a redoubling of effort, as everyone else in the mill had done. They simply ignored him. Not one of the croppers looked up as our party entered the shop; they just carried on working at the same steady competent, confident pace. A human pace, not one dictated by the rhythm of the machines; for they had no machines, only their shears and the tables on which they worked. They were the only people in the entire mill who seemed to be happy in their work.

Even Mr Moore did not look happy as he escorted us to his house near the mill, and introduced us to his sister, Hortense, who kept house for him. The word 'joy' seemed never to have crossed his lips.

Times were hard, he said. The war against the French, which had been dragging on most of my lifetime, had led to the closure of the biggest overseas market, America, because of the Orders in Council (he almost spat out the words) that restricted trade with neutral countries. The demand for cloth for red coats did little to compensate.

'If I understand you,' I said, 'the French, the English and the Americans have no other aim but to ruin you.'

'They each try to starve the others into submission,' Mr Moore said. 'Merchants and manufacturers are driven into destruction, and the only people who profit are smugglers!'

'Yet there are other points of view. You do not show much tolerance for them.' I was impertinent to talk thus on such short acquaintance, but he interested me and I thought this was the best way to draw him out.

'I have little time for tolerance. I have to keep two hundred people in work, and to make a profit. I cannot afford to consult everybody's opinions before I say "Do this" and "Do that".'

'If that is your view, I should perhaps not ask you something which I wanted to know.'

'You are free to ask, Miss Keeldar, so long as I have the freedom to give you an answer you may not like.'

'I'm concerned about the children I saw. Is it necessary for children as young as seven to work so hard? You told me that they start at six in the morning and work until six at night. Is that not too much for those so young?'

'They are not forced to work. Indeed, I have more asking for a place than I have room for. I am not a harsh employer – no child is ever beaten in my mill, and they have their breaks for meals.'

'But they never see the sun!' I cried.

'Do you have a better alternative? Should I simply tell them that there is no work for them? That would not please them, I assure you, nor their parents, who depend on their wages so they don't starve.'

I knew as much political economy as any other young lady of twenty-one: none whatever. But I could not help saying, 'It just seems wrong, that's all.'

'Wrong, Miss Keeldar? When their work helps to pay for the rent on this mill – that goes to you?'

For the first time for a month I went to sleep worrying about something other than the bite of a mad dog.

The fortune that had given me such pleasure came in part from the hard work of children who never saw the sun. I didn't like that. I didn't know what to do about it: as Mr Moore said, they wouldn't thank me if I stopped them working, even if I could. I woke in the morning, as one often does, with at least part of an answer.

Visitors were announced, and I went down to greet them. Mrs Pryor had been entertaining them; she seemed oddly distracted and watchful, but I could see nothing more about them than a perfectly proper welcome to a new arrival from the Rector of Briarfield and his niece.

I had seen Mr Helstone in the pulpit, but I had not so far had much conversation with him. A granite-looking man, about fifty, not tall, but with broad shoulders and chest that added to an appearance that would have suited a soldier better than a priest.

Caroline Helstone seemed a much more comfortable visitor; a little younger than I, she had an elegant figure, pretty fair hair, and gentle eyes that softened the determination in her chin, the only feature she shared with her uncle. She seemed a little pale, and I chided her uncle for making her walk so far: a mile in the cold wind was too much. I thought.

'Fresh air and exercise will do her good,' said Mr Helstone. 'That's all any young woman needs.'

Miss Helstone and I exchanged glances, as if to say that we both knew that any young woman needed rather more than that. 'Perhaps friendship may also be beneficial,' I suggested, and her smile was answer enough. 'I should be most grateful if

Miss Helstone were to bestow her friendship on me. Mrs Pryor, I am sure, will not mind if I express the need for someone of my own age to talk with.'

Mrs Pryor nodded heartily. 'I should be as happy as you, Shirley, if Miss Helstone would do us the honour of visiting us frequently. That is, if Mr Helstone can spare her.'

'Oh, I can spare her readily enough,' said Mr Helstone. 'She has nothing to do at home but sit around and be idle.'

'So, Miss Helstone, if it would please me, Mrs Pryor and your uncle, all it needs is for you to agree. Say you will come often, please!'

'I should love to,' she said with a smile that showed that she had not often had her wishes taken into account, nor been much pressed to give her company as a favour.

I was taking a dislike to Mr Helstone, and, being unwilling to show my prejudice against a man of the cloth, I tried to be more welcoming. I did not, for example, tell him to mind his own business when he questioned me about my religious principles, but reflected that it could be said that it *was* his business.

A third visitor was announced: Mr Moore, in answer to a request I had sent him earlier that morning. The reaction of my other two visitors could not have been in more marked contrast. Mr Helstone greeted him with the minimum of civility, and only a muttered 'Mr Moore'. Miss Helstone, however, almost started up from her seat when he was announced, and a blush spread over her face and gave her a sudden bloom of beauty. *Oh-ho*, I thought. *Is that where the wind lies?* Mr Moore's greeting to her showed affection, but no more: and he returned Mr Helstone's greeting with equal stiffness.

I welcomed him, then said, 'Mr Moore: Christmas is nearly on us. I shall have my dinner at Sir Philip Nunnely's, and it will be excellent. But I'd enjoy it far more if I knew that those who had worked to pay my rent were also enjoying a good dinner.'

'Thank you: I hope I shall,' he replied.

'I was not talking only of you, sir, but of the men, women and children who work at Hollows Mill. Have they not earned a good dinner from me?'

'I pay them a fair wage. If they cannot afford to dine, it is due to their own improvidence. I give them Christmas Day as a holiday: is that not enough?'

'Yet I should like to ensure that all, even the ones with improvident breadwinners, can go to bed on Christmas night full of good food. With your permission, I should like to arrive on Christmas Eve at the mill bearing a chicken for every man, a sack of fine bread and vegetables for every woman, and a rich fat pudding for every child. Will you permit me to do so?'

'What, so they arrive late and stupid for work the next day? I must lose one day's work out of them: you want me to lose two?'

Whether out of charity for the poor or out of a desire to cross Mr Moore, Mr Helstone proved himself my ally. 'An excellent notion. Just like the old days, when the Squire would provide for the festivities for the whole village.'

'Thank you, Mr Helstone. Indeed, I am the Squire of Briarfield, as my father was before. The mere accident of being born a female should not rob me of that right and responsibility, should it?'

'Things have changed from the days when the squire felt able to come between a master and his men,' said Mr Moore. 'We are in the nineteenth century now, not the middle ages.'

'Oh, I forgot to mention: you too have served my interests, and I wished to give you something too, Mr Moore. A month's freedom from paying rent.' If it cost me forty-two pounds for him to let me spend my own money, so be it.

Miss Helstone put out a hand and laid it on Mr Moore's arm. 'Robert,' she asked. 'Can you not allow Miss Keeldar to be generous?'

The mulish look in his eyes vanished, and he gave in to her gentle appeal. So the man did have some softness in him, after all.

Caroline Helstone and I spent a delightful day on the morrow shopping in the large market town of Stilborough, for there was no question that Briarfield could supply us. I wanted to draw her out, away from the dampening influence of her uncle, as she sat beside me as I drove the cart.

Yes, reader, I had bought a cart rather than a lady's carriage as more in accord with my needs, though I had kept my pair of fine carriage horses: I fancied they were embarrassed and humiliated at the plebeian vehicle they drew.

'I must thank you for your intervention with Mr Moore, Caroline,' I said (we were already on Christian name terms). 'He seemed pleased to acknowledge your influence.'

She blushed a little, but spoke composedly. 'We are cousins, you see. My mother was his father's half-sister.'

'Your mother is dead?' I said, as gently as I could.

'Well, I think so.' I looked my surprise at her uncertainty, and it prompted her to add, 'I was taken away from her when I was only a baby. Then, when my father died, she did not come to claim me. So I must presume her dead.'

'And so you went to Mr Helstone. Your father's brother, I presume?'

'Yes. He is no relation to Rob– to Mr Moore, as you must have guessed from their manner.'

'On the contrary, I would have thought from their obvious mutual dislike that they were close kin, whose enmity went back to the nursery.'

She sighed a little. 'It is politics that divides them. My uncle is a High Tory. His allegiance to the King and to the old ways is as strong as to the Church of England, and he makes of them the eleventh and twelfth commandments. My cousin, however, cares nothing for the King, and sees tradition as nothing but a stumbling-block in the way of progress. My uncle calls him a Jacobin: he calls my uncle a reactionary. Isn't that a silly thing to fall out about?'

'I don't share your indifference to politics. One of the few regrets I have in being a woman is that it denies me the vote that my property would otherwise bring me.'

'Why, who would you vote for? Are you a Whig or a Tory?'

'Neither: I should dearly love to vote for Mr Wilberforce! Now there is a man who deserves the support of every free English man and woman, for the way he has fought so hard against slavery.'

'Ah, that's a cause worth fighting for. But my uncle and my cousin agree there: they are both in favour of liberty for the slaves. But in almost every other matter they disagree. You would not quarrel with another person and refuse to have anything to do with him just because of his politics, would you? It is so stupid, and – and – *unfair!*' she finished, real distress in her voice.

'Unfair on you?'

'Yes!' she burst out. 'My uncle refuses to let me visit my cousins. I have been going regularly to Hortense, Robert's sister, for French lessons, and my uncle has now told me I must not go.' Her distress seemed too strong for the loss of a mere French lesson, but I did not presume to press her further.

Instead I proposed that we practised our French together at least once a day. We started at once, though our tutors would not have approved of the content of our conversation, for we gossiped, justifying ourselves by the thought that we were improving our French.

Even Stilborough could not fully supply our requirements, though I spent freely; some of the men at Hollows Mill would have to be content with a joint of beef or ham rather than a chicken, and the good folk of Stilborough would find it difficult to find puddings for their own celebrations.

On Christmas Eve, I drove the provisions, neatly parcelled, to Hollows Mill. Caroline had persuaded her stern cousin Mr Moore (aided, perhaps, by the consciousness of forty-two pounds rent that he need not pay) to close the mill early so that there would be light in the sky as we arrived: and that was a concession indeed, as it grows dark very early in Yorkshire at that time of year.

Ah, I enjoyed it! I felt warm at the consciousness of doing good. I revelled in my ability to be generous. I loved the respectful gratitude of the mill hands as they accepted my bounty. Yes, I was the Squire, and the gruff Yorkshiremen and women acknowledged it.

At least, nearly all of them did. Mr Moore, who perhaps could not bear to see such bounty going in a direction of which he disapproved, had left to go round the mill locking up and ensuring everything was right and tight for the holiday. The machines had stopped and a blessed silence filled the air, so that I could hear the sound of raised voices. Mr Moore emerged, shepherding out some men whom he had found still working: big men, whom I recognized as the croppers.

'But we haven't finished!' I heard one of them say.

'You finish when I say you finish,' said Mr Moore. 'If I give you a few hours off before Christmas, then you take them and be grateful.'

'Aye, we'll take them, but we'll not be grateful.' The man looked at the hams still undistributed. 'And we'll not take your charity, neither,' he said to me.

'And I'll not take your insolence, William Brook!' shouted Mr Moore angrily. 'You insult Miss Keeldar!'

Hastily I intervened. 'Oh, no. Brook and the others have the same right as any other to accept or refuse my gifts. I am not insulted, though' – I turned to Brook – 'I am curious.'

He looked at me with neither hostility nor respect, but as one human being to another. 'We don't need it, Miss Keeldar. Give it to them as does. We've enough to buy our own dinners. Aye, and a mug or two at the inn to drink your health with, and all,' he added, smiling at me to take any sting out of his refusal.

'And though you won't take my gifts,' I said, smiling back, 'permit me at least to wish you all a merry Christmas.'

The men returned the greeting heartily as they strode out of the gate.

'They'll be glad enough of any charity next Christmas,' came Mr Moore's voice in my ear. I jumped, for I had not realized that he stood so close. 'Those – *croppers!*' he added as if it were a deadly insult. 'They think they have me by the throat. But I'll show them. I'll be shot of them all.'

'What do you mean?'

He grabbed my arm, none too gently, and turned me to face the mill itself. 'Listen and look,' he said, pointing. 'Up there, on the top floor, we have the carding-machine. In the old days, they had to card and comb the wool by hand: days upon days of drudgery to do what that machine can do in three hours. And there,' he pointed to the floor below, 'we have the spinning-mules. It used to take four or five women, spinning constantly, to keep one weaver in thread. A mule can produce enough in an hour to keep a weaver busy for a day. And there they sit,' he pointed to the first floor. 'The weavers use the same handlooms that they've always done, for there is no broadloom machine – yet – that can weave wool in the way that it can for cotton: the threads break too easily. But that isn't a problem: I just provide more looms. And I bring the weavers into the mill, rather than have them work in their homes as they used to do, at the expense of much time for the master in going round delivering the yarn and collecting the cloth. There's no shortage of weavers. And no shortage of fullers and teazellers, either,' he said, pointing to the ground floor. 'It doesn't take much skill, and anyone can learn. Wages are low at the moment, so it's not worth getting in a gig mill to replace them.'

Then he pointed to the cropping shop, where the lights burned from where he had ejected the men still working. 'But *there*, that's the Achilles' heel. Those damned croppers – my apologies for my strong language, Miss Keeldar, but it's a gall that frets me daily. It takes seven years' apprenticeship to train a cropper, and seven more to make him a good one, fit to be trusted with the finest weaves. And it's not just any man who can be trained: those shears weigh forty pounds, so they must be strong as well. There are never enough of them. My cloth piles up before them, and I cannot find any more men to clear the blockage. I have to pay them a huge wage: thirty shillings a week to the best of them – I speak of best in their work, not in their character. I have to take their insolence, and their obedience to my orders only when it suits them.'

'They work hard, though: you had to drive them out to stop them working this evening.'

'That's it! They don't work for me, but for themselves. They treat me as though I just happen to pay their wages. They think that I cannot do without them. But I can!' he finished triumphantly. 'I can, and I shall!'

'But how? Unless there is a machine—'

'Ah, there is. There is a beautiful, wonderful machine that can do the work of five of the devils, and it can be tended by a woman at half the wage. Do you know how much it would save me if I installed shearing frames? Five hundred pounds a year! That's a lot of money.'

It was a lot: it was what he paid me for the rent of the mill and the land it stood on.

'There must be a reason why you have not installed them already.'

'Two reasons. The first is that I cannot amass the capital to buy them: times are hard, and there is nothing to spare on saving up. And the second' – I had never until then seen anyone literally grind their teeth in fury – 'the second is those men themselves: they dare to threaten me! The murderous devils say that if I install shearing frames they'll burn down the mill. There are other cowards of clothiers who have given in to their outrageous demands. But I shall not! I refuse to be cowed by their threats. I defy them!'

His fury had abated with his shout of defiance, and he turned to me in some calm. 'But, as I say, I cannot find the capital to do so. It would be a worthwhile investment, Miss Keeldar; I could pay half as much again interest as you are receiving now.'

I did not answer, but walked to the gate, where I stood watching the croppers make their way up the lane to Briarfield. Mr Moore talked sense: I could see it and hear it. But I couldn't feel it in my heart. Instead I saw those fine men, proud of their skill and strength. They were all that was best in our English labouring classes. They seemed to be the heirs of centuries of free yeomanry: the archers of Agincourt, the sailors at the docks with Good Queen Bess against the Armada, the soldiers who fought for Cromwell to defy a king's tyranny.

Could I be part of destroying that? Even if it did make sense?

The croppers were silhouetted against the evening skyline, and in the light of the last sun a man came towards them, and was greeted by them with evident friendship.

A man whom I recognized: he had appeared in my nightmares of mad dogs and hot irons for a month. The man who had risked his life to save me.

I heard Mr Moore's cry of astonishment behind me as I ran up the lane towards the man, but I ignored him. It was a steep climb, and I was panting as I reached the brow of the hill. But the croppers and the man they met had vanished.

I stood alone on the hill as Christmas night fell.

# PART 2

'It's three months since I was bitten, Mrs Pryor,' I said one February morning at breakfast. 'And I'm still alive and healthy.'

'Yes, my dear,' she replied, 'and I am delighted that you're now safe.'

'Not quite safe yet. The doctor gave me nine chances out of ten at this stage. I try not to show it, but I'm still aware of that tenth chance.'

'There are many soldiers who would be very happy to know, before they went into battle, that they had nine chances out of ten of survival.'

'What a wonderful, wise woman you are! You're quite right. All the same, I would dearly love to know that the man who was bitten with me was still alive and healthy too: the doctor said that if he was after three months, I would certainly live. I give you my word, if I see him I'll fling my arms around him and kiss him passionately.'

'I hope not, my dear. He's only a working man.'

'In my view, a fine, strong, good man who risks his life to save a damsel in distress is a knight in shining armour, even if he does wear clogs. And now,' I said, 'Sir Philip has invited us to the Assembly at Stilborough, and I intend to have every eligible gentleman there falling at my feet. I feel disposed to

41

enjoy myself. And I shall order a new dress, since there are nine chances out of ten that I shall wear it again, and it will be the most beautiful dress I have ever bought.'

The Briarfield dressmaker might not have had the reputation of her London rivals, but she had access to their patterns and material, and produced a wondrous confection in peach silk, with tiny seed-pearls applied round the hem, cuffs and the high waist we all wore in those days. I unearthed the cashmere shawl that my uncle had sent me, and the reticule, handkerchiefs and gloves so intricately embroidered by his wife and daughters. Sir Philip's gift of ear-rings matched the pearls round my neck, on my wrist, and in my hair to complete the ensemble. A thick cloak of good Yorkshire wool, lined with silk, kept me warm on the journey. Reader, I hope you will forgive an old woman for these fond reminiscences: it was indeed the most beautiful dress I ever bought.

On the Assembly itself I shall be brief. I was in my best looks, I was young and rich, and I was betrothed to a baronet: I enjoyed myself immensely. I was besieged by requests to dance, and it would have been uncivil to refuse the officers in their regimentals, the clothiers on their best behaviour, and the gallant sons of the West Riding gentry and nobility: and if I confined myself to the handsomest, who is to blame me?

The Assembly Rooms in Stilborough are part of its largest inn, and it was in the inn yard as we prepared to leave that the adventure of the night began.

'Oh, Sir Philip, Mrs Pryor, look!' I cried. 'It's Mr Moore! Pray, let us greet him.' He was standing surrounded by a patrol of the militia, haranguing its officer. I was curious, and determined to find out what the matter was. Sir Philip allowed himself to be persuaded: unwillingly, I know, for on the only occasion the two men had met an instant antipathy had sprung up between them. But Sir Philip was always civil.

Mr Moore was not: he acknowledged us with only the briefest greeting, and continued his tirade. 'You think this parcel of nincompoops is sufficient to defend my property!' he shouted at the officer. 'Look at them. Half-drunk already, and a night's long cold journey ahead of us!'

'The men have been only waiting for you, Mr Moore. They cannot be blamed for waiting in the inn and sampling its comforts.'

'Sampling its comforts!' Mr Moore roared. I thought it was time to interject a little diversion into the scene before he exploded.

'Pray, Mr Moore, will you not tell us what is happening?' I asked hastily. 'Or Captain – er?' I added inquiringly.

With ill grace, Mr Moore introduced Captain Carpenter of the militia, who seemed more disposed to talk to us: no doubt thankful for the relief.

'We are to escort Mr Moore and his shearing-frames over Stilborough Moor to Hollows Mill,' he said. 'There have been threats made, and it is our duty to protect his life and property.'

'So, Mr Moore,' I said. 'You have your frames at last?' Without my financial support, I refrained from adding: my refusal to lend him the capital he needed had caused him some resentment.

'Yes, I have my frames. All it needs is to get them in place, and I'll be free of those damned croppers forever.'

'And the – er – *deuced* croppers are proposing to fight you, I gather.'

Mr Moore pulled from his pocket a grubby sheet of paper, on which was written this illiterate scrawl:

Do not think that you can bring your dam masheens into your mill to distroy mens work and lives. you think your-self a hard man but you will find that Yorkshire men are harder.

Take this warning from
General Ludd.

'Luddites!' I cried. 'So the infection has spread here?'

'Indeed it has,' said Mr Moore. 'And all we have to defend us against this seditious violence are Captain Carpenter and his men,' he sneered. 'Of whom all are drunk, and none knows the way over Stilborough Moor.' For these were not the local militia: the authorities did not trust West Riding men to put down their fellows and had brought in soldiers from another county.

'Well, perhaps we may help, at least on the last point.' I turned to Sir Philip. 'Since our way to Fieldhead lies in the same direction, shall we not act as guides for Captain Carpenter?'

'But . . .' stammered Sir Philip. 'Surely it would be safer for you and Mrs Pryor to come home with me, if these lawless ruffians are known to be at large?'

'Come, Sir Philip, you would not shirk your duty to help the militia?' I turned to the captain. 'We have two pistols in the coach, and the readiness to use them.' After our experience with the misfiring pistol, we had taken to carrying a pair, and ensuring that the powder and shot were always ready to hand.

Mr Moore did not object, and Captain Carpenter seemed grateful for our help, so in just a few minutes we set out in convoy, a couple of soldiers riding ahead, Sir Philip's coach next, some more soldiers following with Captain Carpenter, then Mr Moore and his frames, and two more riders in the rear.

I had all sorts of romantic visions as we drove through the night: I fancied myself as Boadicea, or Hippolyte the Amazon, or any other warlike lady of history. Above all, I did not take it seriously, for I could not see how a handful of labouring men would dare to attack us. Mrs Pryor and Sir Philip were more inclined to worry, but I had survived three months of dread, I'd had every eligible gentleman at the Assembly falling at my feet, and I was in my finest ball-gown. Nothing could possibly go wrong.

From Stilborough to Hollows Mill and Fieldhead is a journey of some ten miles. The first five are over good road and we made quick progress. I noticed Sir Philip looking longingly at the road to his house which led off it: that's when he loaded the pistols. The last five are over rolling moorland, sparsely populated, and the road is at the best of times no more than a rutted and muddy cart track. At night, with only the moon to light our way (and that often obscured by clouds), the journey was trying: we should have gone faster if we'd walked.

We proved our usefulness; Harry the coachman was very familiar with the route, as he had carried Sir Philip to Fieldhead several times a week in the past months. Our carriage lamps were good and illuminated the way for the whole party, except for two mounted men riding well ahead of the lights to keep their night vision. We in the coach were warm, with our coats, blankets and hot bricks, but I did not envy the men outside in the icy February wind over the moor.

We reached the top of a small rise when one of the men who had been riding ahead of us came back at a gallop.

'Look, sir, over there,' I heard him say to Captain Carpenter. 'There's a fire.'

Captain Carpenter rode up to our coach. 'Is that from one of the houses round here?' he asked Harry.

'No, sir,' he replied. 'I've not seen that before.'

'Bristow,' said Carpenter to the rider. 'Take one of the men and go and investigate.'

'Sir,' said Bristow hesitantly. 'If that fire's from the Luddites, I've no chance to catch them with just one man.'

'You're right, man. Take half a dozen, and see how many of the vermin you can round up.'

'Are you mad?' exclaimed Mr Moore. 'What, leave my frames with just a handful of men to guard them?'

The captain hesitated indecisively. As if to give him a sign, the moon came out from behind a cloud and illuminated the valley ahead of us.

'Look, sir,' he said, pointing to the rolling fields where there appeared to be nothing but grass, rocks and sheep. 'There's no band of men in front of us, and none behind us, or we'd have encountered them already. We'll go no further than the next rise, but we'll be safe enough.'

Mr Moore was about to argue, but Bristow had already taken his six men towards the direction of the fire, and soon they were out of sight as well as earshot. Our depleted band moved forward slowly.

We had reached the bottom of the valley when, suddenly, it happened.

There was the sound of men all about us; of feet jumping up on the coach and of the coachman's cry, muffled instantly; of just one shot followed by a thud of a cudgel and a groan; of shouts and curses and blows.

'My God, it's the Luddites!' cried Sir Philip. For a second I saw his face filled with terror, and he saw that I saw it. He gulped, then, motioning me and Mrs Pryor to silence, moved to the carriage window to peer out. He cocked his pistol, started to open the carriage door, and then he was still. 'I can't risk it.'

Then a huge hand pulled open the door, and another huge hand grabbed him and hauled him straight out of the coach.

'Another one here!' shouted his captor, grabbing the pistol and tucking it in his belt.

'Right, tie him up with the others,' came the order. 'Any more in there?'

A face loomed in at the carriage door; at first I thought it was an African, it was so black. Then I realized that the man's face was covered with soot to disguise his features. He seemed enormous: only his pale eyes and crooked teeth showed against the blackness, and he seemed the very devil. For a second I quailed, and Mrs Pryor was terrified. The face pulled back. 'Nowt but a couple of lasses!'

'Bring the man over here, then pick up thine Enoch and start to work, Number Six,' said the voice we'd heard before. 'And thee, Number Thirty-six, keep an eye on the ladies.'

The huge man disappeared with Sir Philip, and was replaced by a very small man. No wonder he's only number thirty-six, I thought: even though face was blackened, he did not seem threatening in comparison with his predecessor.

But Mrs Pryor was not reassured. 'What will happen to us?' she moaned.

'Nothing very much, I think,' I said, holding her hand and trying to comfort her. 'It seems we ladies are to be unmolested. And the fact that Sir Philip and the other men are tied is a good sign, surely. It means that there is no intent on their lives.' She stopped shuddering, and seemed to have recovered the courage that I knew she had.

From outside the coach we could hear the sound of hammering. They were smashing the machines, and Mr Moore's oaths only seemed to drive them on more cheerfully. I heard shouts which I did not then understand: *Enoch makes them! Enoch breaks them!* They were even singing: a song I would come to know very well.

> *Come cropper lads of high renown*
> *Who love to drink good ale that's brown*
> *And strike each haughty tyrant down*
> *With hatchet, pike and gun.*
>
> *Oh, the cropper lads for me*
> *The gallant lads for me,*
> *Who with lusty stroke the shear-frames broke*
> *The cropper lads for me.*

I didn't know how much good brown ale they'd had, but the strokes were exceedingly lusty, and the shear-frames were indeed breaking.

I put my arm round Mrs Pryor, as if to comfort her more, and whispered in her ear, 'Can you summon up a little resolution? I have an idea.' At that, she seemed even more terrified than she had before, but she nodded. 'Move over to the door by our captor, and try to block his view of me. Talk to him, perhaps. Just stop him from looking inside and seeing what I'm doing.'

That brave, wonderful woman. She gulped down her fear and moved towards the door. Our small captor scowled ferociously at her.

'I am just getting a flask of brandy,' she said. 'A lady's nerves—' She stood up, fumbling near the roof of the carriage where the flask was stored.

My moment. Hastily I grabbed the other pistol from its holster. I unfastened my cloak: I did not want its folds to get in my way. I was ready, the pistol concealed in the folds of my beautiful peach-silk dress, and I nodded.

Mrs Pryor sat down again. She took a sip of the brandy herself, then leaned over me.

'My dear, drink some,' she said. 'It will fortify your nerves.' My nerves, I confess, needed fortification at that moment, and I took a small swallow. I returned the flask to Mrs Pryor and gestured to her to get out of my way. One deep breath, and I was ready. I slid carefully along the seat to the open door, where our captor, reassured that we were occupied and harmless, had let his attention wander to the activities of his fellows.

Then I pounced. One hand went round his neck; the other held the pistol to his head.

'One shout and you're a dead man,' I hissed. There was a little squeak of terror from him, but no more. Still holding him firmly, I climbed out of the carriage.

'Stop!' I cried to the men on the wagons. 'Or I shoot this one.' Instantly their hammers dropped. I could see that there were perhaps a couple of dozen of them round the frames, with more guarding their prisoners.

'Untie those men!' I commanded. None of the Luddites moved. 'I mean it!' I gestured menacingly with the pistol, and the little Luddite in my grip gibbered in fear.

The Luddites, after their initial surprise, were no longer looking at me, but at one of themselves: a big man, even among the other big men, of commanding aspect. His face was hidden by a black mask so that only his eyes showed. He jumped down from the wagon, flinging his hammer to one side as if it were weightless, and walked steadily towards me.

'Another pistol. I should have guessed,' he said in the broad Yorkshire accent of all of the men around him.

I gestured again. 'I'll shoot him if you take another step closer.'

'So,' he said. 'We kill children, do we?'

'Children?'

'Have a close look at him, lady.'

I did: and I saw that the Luddite who had scowled so ferociously was a boy who couldn't have been more than eleven. I shuddered at what I had nearly done, and threw him from me with revulsion. But now I pointed my pistol squarely at the big man in front of me.

'Very well: I shall shoot you instead.'

'Aye, and what would that serve? Kill one Luddite and there are thousands more to replace me.'

'I think not,' I said. 'I think that you would be difficult to replace. In fact, I think that you are General Ludd himself.'

He swept off an imaginary hat and bowed low in mock courtesy. 'At your service, lady.'

I raised my voice and called to his men. 'Get off those wagons and untie the prisoners, or I kill your leader!'

'Don't you move an inch!' he called back to his men, his eyes still fixed on me. How strange: there was a definite twinkle in them.

'Kill him!' I heard a cry from Mr Moore.

'Shoot him down!' cried Captain Carpenter.

Then all of the prisoners – except, I think, Sir Philip – were taking up the cry: 'Kill him! Kill him!'

I raised the pistol. I was proud of myself: my hand was not shaking. The man stepped towards me; the shouting died, and there was silence as all eyes watched us.

'Happen you won't,' he said, walking steadily closer.

'I will.'

'Happen the pistol's not loaded.'

'It's loaded.'

'Happen it'll misfire.'

'It'll fire.' Sir Philip had taken good care of his weapons since three months ago, when one of them had misfired. . . .

The man was rolling up his sleeve; casually, it must have seemed to everyone watching, as if he was preparing for work. But there was nothing casual in his eyes as they held mine, then fell upon the scar on his arm.

The scar of a red hot iron. A scar like the one I saw daily on my ankle.

'Happen you won't shoot me down – like a mad dog,' he added, but he didn't need to.

I didn't shoot him, of course. Neither did I fling my arms around him and kiss him passionately. I had to clap my hand over my mouth to stop myself roaring with laughter, as the weight of the tenth and final chance lifted off my back.

He must have been almost as pleased to see me alive and healthy as I was to see him: that was why his eyes had been dancing so merrily. He had the advantage of me: he had a mask over his face, but I could see that his body was shaking.

The sheer incongruity of our meeting: I in my pearls and peach-silk ball-gown, he in his Luddite black mask and working men's clothes. Enemies, with a loaded pistol between us, but united in joy at seeing the other so well, at the lifting of the horror that had hung over us, and at learning that Providence had a sense of humour.

'Kill him! Kill him!' came the shouts of the prisoners again: this instantly stopped my laughter.

I let the pistol fall. 'No, I can't shoot you down,' I said, 'like a mad dog.' I heard the prisoners' groans of disappointment and frustration.

He put his hand out, and I gave him the pistol. Our hands met: and the warm, healthy, and above all *alive* feeling of him was – no, I have not the words to describe that touch. But from the way he held my hand for much longer than he needed to, he felt it too.

He let go of my hand. 'By rights, you and your friend' – he gestured to Mrs Pryor, her head peering out of the coach window – 'should be tied up with the others until yon pack of gormless soldiers comes back, which'll give my lads a chance to get away. But if you give me your word you'll not untie your friends, I'll let you back in the carriage to wait in comfort.'

'I give you my word,' I said. 'Mrs Pryor?' She nodded in agreement, and he handed me back into the carriage.

There was a cry of protest from the Luddites at this.

'We don't make war on women,' he called to them.

'She's a bloody mill-owner!' I heard one of them shout. 'You can't stake our lives on her word.'

'Excuse me,' he said politely. Then he turned back to his men. 'I'll stake more than our lives: I'll stake my brass. Who'll take me on? My money says she'll keep her word.'

I shook my head at the audacity of it, as he calmly went round the men making wagers. They were engaged in a desperate activity, and the troops were coming back any minute. But all the while the smashing continued, they could whistle cheerfully, and make bets on whether I'd keep my word!

Then the destruction was over, and they were off into the night. But before they left, the man in the mask gave me a very broad wink.

> *Oh, the cropper lads for me*
> *The gallant lads for me,*
> *Who with lusty stroke the shear-frames broke,*
> *The cropper lads for me.*

We heard their voices in triumphant song for a long time after we could see them, as they melted back into the moor from which they had arisen so suddenly.

When it was clear that they'd all left, I got out of the carriage.

'Come and untie us!' yelled Mr Moore. 'We can be after them if we're quick.'

'I gave my word not to,' I said. There was a howl of protest, and not only from Mr Moore. 'You heard me give my word!' I said again. 'But we can make you more comfortable while we wait for the other soldiers to come back. Mrs Pryor, bring the blankets and the brandy.'

From the response I got from Mr Moore as I threw a blanket over his still-tied form, I don't think he was very grateful.

I whistled cheerfully as I came down to breakfast next morning.

'My dear,' said Mrs Pryor reproachfully.

'Thank you, my darling, proper Mrs Pryor,' I said. 'You are right: whistling is most unladylike, and I need you to remind me of it.'

'It's not just *that* you were whistling. It's *what* you were whistling.'

Oh dear. That catchy little tune that I had heard last night had somehow twisted itself into my memory: *The cropper lads for me* was a most inappropriate song for a mill-owner.

How good everything was that morning! The boiled eggs had a new savour, Mrs Pryor's demure neatness was fresh and beautiful, the old oak panelling had lost its gloom, and the February greyness promised nothing but spring.

Sir Philip had stayed the night with us, fatigue and compassion for his coachman having won out over propriety. As he entered the room I jumped up to greet him and kissed him heartily.

'My love!' he cried, surprised and delighted, as he returned my embrace with vigour. 'Why so cheerful this morning?'

I should tell him, I knew. I wanted to shout to the world that I was free of the dread that had been with me for three months, colouring everything I did and said.

But if I told him, then there would be no reason to delay our marriage.

A comforting excuse sidled into my mind. Of course I could not reveal to anyone that the man who had risked his life for me was none other than General Ludd: it would be monstrous ingratitude to inform against the man, wouldn't it?

I looked at Sir Philip's kind, loving face. 'Yours was not among those voices shouting at me to kill; and you applauded the way I kept my word, though it meant I had to leave you tied up in discomfort. I have learned what a gentle, honourable man I am engaged to,' I said, and I was sincere about it. Nevertheless, I was glad I still had my excuse to delay our wedding.

The rector and Caroline were announced. They had come for – *gossip*, I was about to say, but, in deference to Mr Helstone, I must call it *news*. All Briarfield was discussing what had happened last night, and Mr Helstone wanted to find out more than mere rumour could tell him.

We were in the middle of relating the events to our visitors when Mr Moore arrived. He looked worn and grim, as if he had not had the benefit of a good night's sleep. Neither Mr Helstone nor Sir Philip welcomed his arrival: Caroline clearly did. He ignored both chill and warmth, and spoke to me directly. 'Miss Keeldar, may I have a few moments of your time in private?'

I took him into the garden where we could not be overheard. Snowdrops were braving the weather, and even a few daffodils were starting to shoot, with so much more of the sun and so much less of the wind than their fellows outside the sheltering walls. I could leave my guests to entertain each other: Mrs Pryor and Caroline were always pleased to see each other, and Sir Philip's politics were not far removed from Mr Helstone's.

Mr Moore took a little time to begin. 'Last night,' he said eventually, 'I may have behaved towards you – indeed, I know I did – most discourteously. I was churlish, Miss Keeldar, and I apologize.'

It took a lot for that stern, proud man to apologize, and I liked him for it.

'I reproached you for keeping us in our bonds. I should not have done. If that Luddite scum knew that a lady keeps her word, then I should too. I am ashamed: if you will forgive me, it will be easier for me to forgive myself.'

'I forgive you heartily, Mr Moore.'

'Thank you, Miss Keeldar. All I could see last night was that I was being ruined, and helpless to prevent it. Yes, I wanted you to shoot. Then this morning I reflected that *we* had failed: I, whose property it was, and Carpenter and his soldiers, whose duty it was. How could I blame you for not coming to my rescue? If I may say so, you would have been far more of a mill-owner if you had killed that man, but you would have been far less of a woman.'

Fifty years later, I acknowledge your acuteness, Robert Moore. You saw then what I had not even begun to realize myself: the conflict between the mill-owner and the woman.

'You spoke of ruin?' I asked, concerned. 'Is it in truth as bad as that?'

'Yes,' he said, his face not moving. 'I took a gamble, and I lost. I needed those frames. The mill can't continue paying five hundred pounds a year to keep the croppers. So I went into debt, knowing that I could pay it off in three years, or even less if trade looks up. But now – I have no way to repay it, and I am ruined.'

I suspected that this was the real reason for his visit, not to apologize to me. But I did not blame him: he was desperate.

'Forget the woman,' I said, 'and look only at the mill-owner. You're a good tenant, and I'm willing to help you. Besides, there are two hundred jobs in the mill, and Briarfield will starve if it loses them. How much interest are you paying on the debt?'

'Twelve per cent.'

'I shall take over your debt, and you need pay me only six: that's more than I get at the moment, so you'd do me a favour if you accepted. You need not worry that I shall press you hard for repayment, if I know you are doing your best.'

'Ah, I knew you would say that. I knew your generosity of spirit. But I cannot take it. I should be defrauding you. I could not even pay the interest, let alone the capital, without those frames.'

'And if you brought in new frames?'

'Yes, then I could manage.'

'If you could keep them safe from the Luddites.'

'Damn them!' He made no apology for his language: he had

forgotten the woman for the mill-owner. 'And some of them my own men!'

'You know that? How could you recognize any of them last night?'

'One of them called out that you were a mill-owner: how could he know that unless he worked in your mill and had seen you? That's not all: I went into the cropping shop this morning. And they just smiled at me: no friendly smile, but a knowing one, laughing at my discomfiture. And one of them had the cheek to whistle that damned Luddite song.'

I was thinking hard. On the one hand were two hundred jobs, and Robert Moore: hard-working, stern, honest. On the other were a few croppers, and a man who'd risked a horrible death for me.

'This is not a decision to be made lightly and without investigation,' I said at length. 'With your permission, I shall have my lawyer look at your figures. But if things are as you say, you'll have your frames. You have my word on it.'

There was no surprise at the message: I had been waiting for it. I'd half expected it to appear mysteriously on my pillow, or through some other romantic means, but instead it came through the prosaic medium of the Post Office.

*Robin Hoods tower. noon. friday.*

Not a man to waste words, I thought as I looked at the unformed hand, more used to wielding a hammer than a pen. I felt flattered that he saw no need to tell me that I should go alone.

We of the West Riding have our share in Robin Hood: indeed, we think many of the Nottinghamshire tales of Sherwood Forest are a little fraudulent. The Briarfield legend said that a woman had brought his doom to him here on Stilborough Moor, and he'd died, defiant to the end.

I climbed down from the cart and hitched the horses to an old tree. I looked around: I seemed to be alone. And then, there he was.

We said nothing for a while, but stared at each other in silence. I don't know what he saw, but now I had light and calm to study him clearly, I saw a massive man in his late twenties – not handsome, no gentleman – in a rough coat and corduroy trousers, his shirt open at the top to show a strong neck and chest. The jacket was too short for his arms, and revealed his wide wrists, firm and gnarled like a tree branch. The hands: great, brawny, working men's hands, used to toil, with the croppers' mark – the weal across the wrist and base of the hand from those forty-pound shears. I hadn't seen it before at the smithy, because my attention had been on his other arm, where he had been bitten. And on his eyes, the ones that had held mine and given me courage to cauterize my wound, and had laughed so merrily the other night. And on him: not what he looked like, but what he was.

'To think that I risked my life for a mill-owner!'

'To think that I owe my life to a Luddite!'

Then – I don't know which of us began it – we laughed. Great, howling, gulping laughter that made our eyes stream and left us breathless and shaking.

'You – with that mask over your face . . .' I gasped.

'And you, with the pistol in your hand in yon pretty dress . . .'

'And all those voices, shouting, "Kill him, kill him"!'

'Hey, lady, that weren't funny,' he said, suddenly sober.

'No, it wasn't. Not at the time.'

'Did you get into strife for not shooting me?'

'Not much. They've decided that, after all, I'm only a poor, weak woman, who couldn't possibly be expected to have the resolution to shoot a man down.'

He laughed again. 'They don't know you.'

'No, they don't. I would have killed you if you hadn't been – you.'

'Aye, I know that. I saw it in your face as I were coming toward you. And I thought, happen she'll know me, or happen she won't, but at least I'll die laughing. And when you did recognize me – well, you should have seen your face: it were a treat to behold.'

'I've never been happier in my life to see anyone. The doctor told me that if you were alive and healthy after three months, then I had nothing more to worry about. And there you were, so splendidly alive and healthy, and that horrible fear left me. You know – you must have felt it too: the knowledge that you could die insane and screaming.'

'Lady, I recollect that often enough without you reminding me.' I saw him shudder. Then he smiled and changed the subject. 'I've brought you your winnings. Five pound I collected on you keeping your word: here's your half.'

It was on the tip of my tongue to tell him to keep it: I didn't need the money. But I realized that he needed to give it to me. 'Thank you,' I said, and held out my hand.

Then I realized what he had just done.

'You were testing me!' How dared he? How did he have the impertinence to patronize me like that? Then I caught myself thinking *It should be me that patronizes him.*

'Well, tha passed, lady,' he said, and I laughed as he held my hand and counted two pounds ten shillings into it. It was absurd for a lady like me to feel gratified at the approval of the leader of a gang of Luddites, and to welcome a working man using the intimate *tha* rather than the respectful *you*, and to gain such glowing pleasure from the touch of that great calloused hand. But I did. And he appeared to like the touch of my hand too, for again he kept it for longer than he needed to before he let it go.

'I wish you wouldn't call me *lady*: I have a name.'

'Oh, aye, I know that right enough. But I can't think of thee as *Miss Shirley Keeldar of Fieldhead*. I think of thee as a lady: not like them primping, precious ladies you see in *Society*' – he said the word with scorn – 'but as what a lady ought to be: brave, true, beautiful.'

'Well,' I said, feeling ridiculously flattered, 'you have the advantage of me. You may think of me as a lady, but I don't want to think of you as a Luddite, and I don't know your name.'

He hesitated.

'Oh, come now. You just said I was a true lady. You cannot possibly believe that I would inform on you, with what I owe to you.'

'Tom,' he said. 'Mr Thomas Mellor, of – of Robin Hood's Tower.'

'I fancy you think of yourself as Robin Hood, don't you? An outlaw, robbing the rich to give to the poor.'

He began to sing, in a rich brown voice:

> *'Chant no more of your old rhymes about bold Robin Hood,*
> *His feats I but little admire.*
> *I will sing the achievements of General Ludd,*
> *Now the hero of Nottinghamshire.*

– but that's not a West Riding song, though we've as much claim to Robin Hood as the Notts lads have.'

'General Ludd, the hero of Nottinghamshire, are you? I shouldn't have thought it of a Yorkshireman like you.'

'Nay, that weren't me. General Ludd's nobbut the name we put at the bottom of letters. Tha was wrong, the other night, when tha said that I couldn't be replaced. I could name thee six men who could take over from me, right here in the West Riding. But I shan't, of course, you being a mill-owner.'

'You don't trust me?'

'Thee, I trust with my life. But I'll not trust other men's lives to a mill-owner.'

'You already have, when you left me untied and gambled on my word.'

'Nay, that weren't gambling. That were betting on a certainty. But I couldn't pass up the chance of making a bit of brass.'

'I think, Mr Thomas Mellor of Robin Hood's Tower, that you are an unscrupulous rogue.'

'Aye, that's me,' he acknowledged cheerfully. 'And *a seditious agitator* and *a treasonous rebel who leads poor ignorant fools into riot,*' he added, mimicking the accents of those who had described the Luddite leaders thus. 'Lady, we're *enemies*, thee and me. We were bitten by the same mad dog, but that don't make us blood brother and sister, now, do it?'

'I don't want to be your enemy.'

'And God knows I don't want to be thine. But we are, all the same.'

'So be it. I shall fight your cause with everything I have. But I shall not do anything to harm you.'

'I'll meet thee on thy terms: I'll fight for the Ludds, but I'll not hurt thee.'

The word *meet* hung in the air. Did he mean it literally or metaphorically? I couldn't ask him that: he probably wouldn't understand the words. But though he might not be able to read books very well, he could read faces superbly, for he said after a long moment of silence, 'Aye, I mean *meet*. Dost tha want us to?'

He was an ill-educated working man: a rebel against the law and against all the principles I'd been taught. But he'd risked his life to save mine, and he was by far the most intriguing person I'd met since I'd come to Briarfield: come to think of it, he was the most intriguing person I'd met in my life.

'Yes, I do. And you?'

'Aye. I must be mad, wanting to have more to do with a mill-owner than I need to, but I do.'

He held my hand, and again I felt that feeling of aliveness flowing from him. I was beginning to blush, so I took my hand away hastily and changed the subject.

'I don't think that either your people or mine would be happy about it if they found out.'

'Tha's not wrong there,' he said, with a fervour that told me he was thinking of the reactions of his comrades if they knew he was meeting a mill-owner in secret.

'How shall we arrange to meet?'

'There's nowt wrong with the Post Office. I'll write to thee, or tha can write to me at The Shears,' he said, naming the croppers' inn, a notorious Luddite haunt. 'Your folk will open the letter, and mine'll read it, so write nobbut the day, and we'll meet here at noon.'

'Yes, but what name shall I use? Surely not General Ludd or Tom Mellor.'

There was a twinkle in his eye. 'What about – Beau Brummell?'

I burst out laughing, for there could be no more marked contrast between that elegant dandy and this man in his worn coarse clothes. 'You'll be setting a fashion for clogs!'

He gave a rich, deep chuckle at the idea. And I thought, *How rare, how delightful it is: we make each other laugh.*

With Mr Pearson's report in my hand, I strode down to Hollows Mill. There were no lights in the mill except in the counting-house, which told me that Robert Moore was there, working late, as ever.

As I approached the mill gates a ferocious barking arose, and two large dogs raced up snarling. I was, understandably, still somewhat afraid of dogs, and I waited by the gate until the door of the counting-house opened and Robert Moore's tall figure was silhouetted against the light.

'Down, Tartar. Down, Hannibal.' He opened the gate for me, and the dogs, beautifully trained, ceased their growls. I held out my hand for them to sniff: we were friends.

'Do they always make friends so easily?' I said as he escorted me to the counting-house. 'If so, I fear that your enemies will suborn your guards.'

'They're well trained,' he said. 'And they don't attack women.'

'I approve of such chivalry: of dogs and Luddites that don't harm women.'

'Luddites, hah!' he said with loathing. 'Scum! Vermin! I'd see the lot of them hanged. And, by God, if this law goes through, that's what I shall see.'

'Law?'

'It makes frame-breaking a capital offence. It'll pass, don't worry. It's going through parliament right now.'

He offered me coffee and cakes from his neat little store in the counting-house, and we set down to business. It did not take long: Mr Pearson's report indicated that the situation was much as Robert Moore described it. The future of the mill hung in the balance. If trade improved – if, for example, the Orders in Council were repealed and the clothiers could sell their goods in America – then prosperity was assured. If not, then the only way to keep going was to turn off some of the workers or reduce their wages, and to install shearing-frames to eliminate the need for highly paid croppers.

As I had no power to repeal the Orders in Council, there was only one thing I could do: keep my word to him.

'You shall have your frames. I'll have Mr Pearson draw up the agreement for the loan.'

The relief on his face was evident. 'Thank you, Miss Keeldar.'

'However, there is a condition. I shall not throw good money after bad. I will need to be assured that you can get the frames in safely, and that they will be protected by more than a couple of dogs.'

'I'm making my plans. A handful of my men are loyal: the ones with brains enough to know that their jobs depend on it. And I have the assurance of Captain Carpenter that the militia will be on hand, and rather better prepared than they were last time.'

As he took me back to the gate, I asked, 'By the way, Mr Moore, who or what is Enoch?'

'Enoch?'

'You remember, surely: "Enoch makes them! Enoch breaks them!" '

We were outside the mill now: he kept the dogs in by closing the gates. 'Yes: it must be Enoch Taylor and his brother James. They have an iron-foundry near Halifax that makes the frames.'

'And perhaps a foundry also makes hammers?'

'It could, certainly.'

'So, we have a man who sells frames to the clothiers, and hammers that break them to the Luddites.' I began to laugh. 'And that, of course, means that he sells more frames to the clothiers, and then more hammers to the Luddites. My word, there are some rogues in the West Riding!'

He was outraged. 'By God, I'll have the law on him!'

'No, you won't, sir. He could do it without stepping a foot outside the law. "Happen tha'll be wanting a dozen hammers for next Tuesday" that's all he'd need to say. All the same, I think you should order your frames from someone else.'

He took my hand in his. 'Miss Keeldar, may I say that I have never seen your equal for intelligence as well as generosity? A man's mind and a woman's heart: it's a rare combination.'

'Why, thank you.' His handshake was cold, hard, unyielding. 'I am flattered.' But not touched, I thought, comparing his grip with another's. I smiled up at him. 'And I have the warmest admiration for you. I think we shall work well together.'

There was a noise – a human sound – from the grove of trees beside the mill.

'Someone's watching us!' he said, dropping my hand and starting after the sound. But he could find no one: if there had been anyone there, they had gone.

'We've learned our lesson,' he said. 'We must, in future, ensure that our plans cannot be overheard. God send that there was no harm done tonight.'

It was only the argument that kept us warm as we stood by Robin Hood's Tower in the howling Yorkshire wind and rain. His jacket and my umbrella gave us little protection as we stood in the lee of the cart, huddled – a very careful huddle in which we did not actually touch – against the weather.

'I wish I could make thee see that it's wrong to destroy people's jobs.'

'I wish I could make you see that it's wrong to destroy people's property.'

'If that's what it takes to save men's livelihoods, then I'll do it!'

'You can't save them! I've seen the figures. Mr Moore can't afford to keep the croppers on – he'd be ruined, and two hundred jobs would be lost at the mill. You're losing other people's jobs, not saving them.'

'Then why are those two hundred people on our side, all but a handful of scabs? We're fighting for their rights, and they know it.'

'But you're getting in the way of progress!'

'Progress? I thought progress were about making people's lives better.'

'It will in the end. Hollows Mill can produce cheap warm clothes for everyone.'

'Aye, everyone who's in work; the rest must freeze. Because what it really produces is profit for Moore and rent for his landlord. If that's progress, I'll have nowt to do with it.'

'Why shouldn't I get rent? I own the land, and my father built the mill. That's my property!' Our voices were becoming raised.

'And a cropper's skill is his property! Aye, and he did summat more to earn it than getting born to the right father. Twelve year it took me to get as good as I am, and I learn fast. It's more like fourteen for the croppers at Hollows Mill.'

'Well, I'm sorry. But just because you worked hard at your trade, that doesn't mean you can expect someone to pay you for it.'

'We've a *right* to work!' he shouted. 'Aye, and to decent wages, that'll allow a man enough to feed his family!'

'Nobody has a right to work!' I shouted back.

'Yes, we do! Or we did, before the law and the mills took it away from us. Oh, damn this!' he said in disgust, moving away from me. 'We're wasting our time. We'll neither of us convince the other one.' He started to walk away.

I was suddenly even colder and wetter as I lost the protection of his massive body against the weather, and it made me realize how sorry I'd be if I never saw him again.

'It would be a waste of time,' I said, in a far more gentle tone than I'd used before, 'if that was the reason we were here.'

He stopped dead, the rain pouring off him, dripping from his hair on to his wide shoulders, making his shirt cling to his body, as I continued, 'I could be in front of a warm fire at home, and I'm sure you could too. We'd both be in trouble with our own people if they knew we were meeting. You didn't come here for an argument about the rights and wrongs of frame-breaking any more than I did.'

He turned back slowly, and looked me up and down, and I knew as he did that the rain made my dress cling to my body too. If any other man looked at me in such a way I should have been insulted, but he was seeing a woman rather than a mill-owner, and I liked it. 'Aye,' he said after a moment. 'Tha's in the right about that, if nowt else.' He smiled as he returned to the protection of my umbrella, and his smile went straight to my heart.

I looked up at his bright blue eyes and smiled back. 'Why did you come?'

'I like to be with thee,' he said simply. 'Happen it's the same for thee?'

'Yes, it is.'

'Show me thy hand.' I did; he held out his, close to mine but not touching. 'Look at thine: small, soft, ladylike. Look at mine: big and work-worn.'

'So let's not look at them,' I said, putting mine in his. 'Let's just hold them.'


I woke, sweating, hot, and flushed with shame and embarrassment. Thanks be to God, I thought, our dreams are private.

He had figured in my dreams often before: but in a nightmare confusion with mad dogs, hot irons, and screaming insanity. This was a dream of a very different kind. No nightmare – I should have preferred the nightmare – but one in which his mouth was on mine, his huge coarse hands were all over my body rousing the feeling that his touch always did, and his words were in my ear: *brave, true, beautiful.*

I got out of bed and washed my face in the nearly frozen

water from the jug. Dawn was just coming up: it was early March, and spring was nearly upon us.

I was revolted with myself. How often had I giggled over the gossip that Lady This had run off with the apothecary's assistant, or Miss That had eloped with the footman. How much I had despised such foolish women. For they had betrayed their class. They had justified all the restrictions and prohibitions placed on women to stop us behaving so.

Was I one of them? Could I fall so easily into the same trap?

I summoned up my resolution and bluntly asked myself the question that my dream had raised: *did I want to lie with him?*

Coolly I surveyed my mental image of the man. He had risked a horrible death to save me: certainly a reason for admiration and gratitude. He made me laugh. I liked to be with him.

Anything more? No! Never! In the light of day, the thought of his hands on my body filled me only with horror.

But it would be wise to ensure that we did not touch in our future meetings.

Perhaps it would be wise to ensure that there were no future meetings.

# PART 3

'Miss Helstone has not been to visit us these four days,' said Mrs Pryor. 'I am worried about her: do you think she is well?'

'You always are worried about her. You make sure she is wrapped up, that she has someone to walk home with her, that she is well-nourished.'

'I think that not enough people have taken care of her,' she replied, a little flustered. 'Certainly not her uncle.'

'Yet he does his duty by her.'

'You do not need me to tell you how little nourishment we get out of duty: what a thin gruel it is to feed a young woman's heart.'

'Very well. I'll visit her: not out of duty, but because we both want her.'

The March afternoon was blustery as I walked to the Rectory. Mr Helstone was not at home, for which I was thankful: Miss Helstone was, but she seemed as if she would have denied me. She looked ill. No, not ill, but as if some light inside her had died. She was polite as she poured out our tea, and she responded to my chatter civilly enough. But she looked as if she wanted me to be gone.

You may have noticed, reader, that I like people to like me, and that I go out of my way, even with such stony men as Mr

Helstone and Mr Moore, to ensure that they do. How much more would I exert myself for gentle, lovable Caroline? She was rather stony herself that afternoon, and it took me a good fifteen minutes for her to acknowledge that no, she was not ill, but that yes, there was something troubling her.

'You will not tell your friend Shirley what it is? You will not confide in one who loves you very much?' She turned away with a gesture of pain. There was only one thing I knew which could cause that. 'It's Robert Moore, isn't it? He has made you suffer.' She made no response. 'I'd like to shoot him!' I said. 'Since you have no one else who'll call him out, I shall. Captain Keeldar will go get her pistols and find a second to issue a challenge to him!'

'Oh, don't jest about it. I know – I know that I must not even think of coming – of coming between you.'

'Of coming between us? Between whom, pray?'

'Between you – and Robert.'

'Me and Robert? Good heavens, where did you get that idea?'

'Oh, Miss Keeldar, I know you love him, and I know he loves you, and I know I am nothing to him and that you are truly worthy of him as I am not. But for God's sake, don't lie to me.'

'What's this *Miss Keeldar* nonsense? I am your Shirley, as ever was. And as ever was, on my honour, there is nothing between me and Robert Moore that can give you any cause for pain.'

'I saw you!' she burst out. 'Last Thursday, outside the mill gates. You were talking, and he held your hand and bent his head towards you in admiration.'

'We knew someone was watching us! Thank God, it was only you!'

'Yes, it was *only me*.'

'Oh, Caroline, I didn't mean it like that, you know I didn't. We feared it might be one of the Luddites, for we were talking too loud about something we should not have been. But what were you doing there?'

'I often do it: walk out from the Rectory at night and look down at the mill. I sometimes even see him, and gain a little comfort from that. You won't tell him, will you?'

'What, betray your secret? No, of course I shan't. But listen to me. I swear to you that there is nothing of that sort between me and your Robert Moore.'

'He's not my Robert Moore.'

'Perhaps not. But he's not mine, either. He's married to his mill: and that's what we were talking about – his only true love. If he was looking at me with admiration and gratitude, and holding my hand, it was because I had saved him and his love. He'd have done the same if it was Mr Rothschild who had come to his rescue – well, perhaps he wouldn't have held Mr Rothschild's hand. It was business, Caroline, *business*. That's all.'

'That's all?' she said: she desperately wanted to believe me.

'That's all, on my word. And I don't break my word. In any case, how could you believe that of me? You know that I am betrothed to Sir Philip Nunnely.'

'I know that you do not love Sir Philip Nunnely.'

'You mustn't say that! Of course I love him.'

'Oh, Shirley, are you lying to yourself or to me? I know how a woman acts when she loves a man, God knows I do. And you don't act like that towards him.'

I stood up. 'You should not have said that.' I turned to go, but she put out her hand to stop me.

'Shirley, you listen to me now. You have brought me happiness this afternoon: not much, but some. Let me do you a service in return. Let me show you that you would be making a mistake, a dreadful mistake that you would regret for the rest of your life, if you married Sir Philip.'

'Why, pray?' I asked stiffly, still about to go.

'Don't you see it? It's so clear to me. When I thought that you and Robert – it gave me such pain, but at least I could think that my friend and my love were worthy of each other. But Sir Philip is no more worthy of you than – than—' she sought for a comparison '—oh, than General Ludd.'

'Oh, Caroline!' I turned back to her, and embraced her. 'Those soft eyes of yours are far too sharp.' She returned my embrace. 'Friends again?'

'Friends again.'

'Caroline, we must not let this man come between us again. Believe me, I love you far more dearly than I love Robert Moore.'

'Or Sir Philip Nunnely?' she enquired gently.

I sat down again: she poured us some more tea. I needed someone to confide in.

'The truth is, Caroline, that I love you and Sir Philip equally – and in exactly the same way. You are both well-informed, good-natured, honest people, worthy of my highest regard. His embrace gives me as much pleasure as yours did just now. And not a jot more.'

'There is no – no *passion* there?'

'None whatever. I do not blush when he comes into the room, as you do with Robert Moore. I would not shed a tear if I thought he loved someone else, nor would I stay away from my best friend. The thought of watching outside his house at night, waiting for a glimpse of him: it's absurd! In truth' – I gave an uncertain laugh; she had no idea how true it was – 'General Ludd rouses more passion in me than he does!'

'Then you must not marry him.'

'Who, General Ludd? I know that.'

'Don't be silly, Shirley. You must not marry Sir Philip.'

'And yet he is kind and gentle, and he loves me.'

'That's not enough for you.'

'Mrs Pryor would disagree with you: she thinks that's quite enough.'

'I think Mrs Pryor has had experience of something else: something that tells her that those qualities are very valuable. She is so kind and gentle and loving herself, isn't she?'

'Yes, she is. And she has been worried about you. Come: let us go to Fieldhead, and let her see that we are friends.'

When we arrived back at Fieldhead, Sir Philip was there, his face full of panic. Caroline pressed my hand, as if to reassure me that she would no more betray my secret than I would hers.

'Shirley, Shirley!' he cried as we entered. 'Thank God you're back.'

'Whatever's the matter?'

'Look at this.' He produced a letter, on the finest notepaper, written in beautiful calligraphy that only a professional secretary could produce.

*Earl Fitzwilliam, Lord Lieutenant of the West Riding, presents his compliments to Sir Philip Nunnely, and would be more than grateful if Sir Philip would assist him in a matter of the highest importance.*

*Earl Fitzwilliam is aware that Luddism has spread to the West Riding. He wishes to meet all those who share his interest in putting down these outrages. He therefore would be in considerable debt to Sir Philip if he would offer the hospitality of his house for such a meeting. Earl Fitzwilliam suggests that a date just before Easter would be convenient. Earl Fitzwilliam would be further indebted if he and his party can be accommodated at Sir Philip's house on the nights before and after the meeting.*

*A list is appended of all those whom Earl Fitzwilliam thinks should be present: Sir Philip may wish to invite any others.*

'What am I going to do?' he cried. 'Earl Fitzwilliam! In my house! I can't cope! Neither can Mamma! And all these others invited – look at the list, there must be thirty names on it!'

I sat him down and gave him a cup of tea.

'Well, the first thing you do, my love, is to write back and say you would be honoured to assist in any way possible. You would be, wouldn't you?'

'Oh, yes, of course. It's a great honour indeed. But—'

'And then give me a chance to read this list – stop waving it around like a madwoman's fan. Ah, yes, Mr Helstone and Mr Moore: they're both down. You go and visit either of those, and ask for their advice about whether this list is complete or whether you should suggest some more names.'

'Mr Helstone,' he said hurriedly. He did not like Mr Moore.

'Then, once you know how many people are coming, and how many people are likely to stay the two nights, you and your Mamma leave all the other arrangements to me.'

'Oh, Shirley! Thank you, thank you, my darling!'

'Don't thank me: I should rather thank you. I have always nurtured an ambition to be a political hostess: this is my apprenticeship. It will be a great success. Leave it to Captain Keeldar.'

We discussed a few other details, then I turned to Mrs Pryor and Caroline. 'And Captain Keeldar will need her two trusty lieutenants.'

They both looked aghast.

'Me?' said Mrs Pryor. 'Good heavens, I couldn't attend such a gathering. Me, a governess, with Earl Fitzwilliam?'

'Oh, Shirley, I've no head for organization,' said Caroline.

'You must come: I need you, both of you. For if it is to be a success, we must invite, not only these worthy gentlemen' – I waved the list – 'but their equally worthy wives. And I can't think of anyone better than you two kind, lovable women to entertain the wives.'

And Caroline might meet a kind, lovable man to put the thought of Robert Moore out of her head.

\*

*Blessed are the peacemakers: for they shall be called the children of God.* I would be a peacemaker: I would find out exactly what the Luddites wanted, what it would take to make them give up their riot. I would carry that message to the meeting, for one way to stop Luddism would be to find some compromise, some means of living together.

So of course I was only doing my patriotic and Christian duty when I wrote: *Beau Brummell, The Shears, Hightown: Wednesday.*

And of course it was the stiff March wind that had reddened my face when I drove the cart up to Robin Hood's Tower at noon.

I am in control of my imagination, I told myself. This is the enemy: a brave enemy to whom I owe my life: but the enemy still. And he is just a working man, with working man's hands and working man's clothes. He would no doubt be shocked if he knew how he had appeared in my dream – dreams, rather, since they had recurred more than once.

Then I felt a blush spread all over me as the thought occurred that perhaps I figured in his dreams in the way he did in mine.

'No, I can manage,' I said, waving aside the hand that he offered to help me down from the cart. 'They haven't hanged you yet, I see,' I said as I alighted and faced him, wishing that the look he was giving me was more like that of an enemy, and less like that of a man towards a woman.

'Nay, the bill's not yet passed that'll make it death to break a frame. But it will pass: there's nowt to stop it.'

'You're not afraid of hanging?'

'Compared with the death that I feared for months, hanging's easy. I don't think I'll ever fear death again. I don't need to tell thee that, surely. Tha felt the same fear.'

'Yes, I did. And I'm no more afraid of death for myself than you are. But I am afraid of it for others. And we can do something to stop it, you and I. That's why I wanted to see you.'

'Oh, aye? And there were me thinking it were for my bonny blue eyes.'

They *were* blue. I couldn't meet them as I said, 'This is much more important than your blue eyes. There is to be a meeting: if you swear you'll not use this information to disrupt it, or to strike against any of the people attending it, I'll tell you more.'

He thought a moment, then said, 'Aye, I swear.'

'It is to discuss Luddism, to try to put it down. And I thought: well, one way to put it down is to give you what you want. That'd stop you dead, wouldn't it?'

'With amazement, aye.'

'But at least make sure that they know what it is that you want.' He looked sceptical, so I tried again. 'I'm a mill-owner. You're a Luddite. We're both prepared to fight for what we want. But surely it's better if we don't have to? There's been blood shed already: there'll be more – from your side and mine – if we don't stop it.'

Unwisely I put out my hand in a plea. He took it – with the usual effect on me.

'Lady, we've tried,' he said resignedly. 'If they don't know what we want, it's not for lack of us telling 'em. We raised hundreds of pounds out of poor men's pockets to send a delegation to parliament: and what did it get us? Nowt save being accused of sedition.' I was hanging my head to hide my blushes, but he must have thought it was in sorrow. 'Oh, very well,' he sighed. 'I'll do what tha wants. Mind, it's not because I think it'll do a ha'porth of good. It's because – I want to please thee.'

There was a note in his voice that made me glad of the excuse to turn away from him and reach into the cart for my neat little portable writing desk. I sat on a tree-stump and placed the desk on my knee.

'Now—' I had to cough: my voice was not completely under my control. 'Now,' I began again. 'This is my idea. Write a letter from General Ludd to Earl Fitzwilliam, telling him what you want. I'll see that he reads it. He's the one who's called this meeting, and I'm in charge of the arrangements.'

'We are mixing with the mighty, aren't we? Tha'd best write it, then. I'll not shame thee by giving thee my handwriting to deliver to an earl.'

'Well, let's start like this: "General Ludd presents his compliments to Earl Fitzwilliam, Lord Lieutenant of the West Riding, and respectfully suggests –" '

'Tha means that I must be respectful to an earl?' he broke in, outraged, then sighed. 'Ah, the thing a man'll do for a pretty woman!'

'– and respectfully suggests",' I continued, ignoring his comment, ' "that if he wishes to end General Ludd's reign, then he should ensure that—" Now, what should he do? What would it take for you all to put down your Enochs and go home?'

'Send the Prime Minister and the Prince Regent to the guillotine, tha means? Oh, aye, Fitzwilliam's bound to take notice of that.'

I looked up at him. 'I'm sorry, but I don't believe you want that. In fact, I think you'd lead a rescue party to the tumbrels and help them escape.'

'Nay, I'm not that daft. But I'd not celebrate if their heads rolled: I'm not a revolutionary. There's Ludds that are, though. Mind, there's others that think of nowt except saving their jobs.'

'Well, what do *you* want? You and those who think like you.'

'It's a long list. Tha's got plenty of paper? Right, then. No more poverty. Lower the price of bread. Raise wages. Make sure that a man can earn enough to feed his family.'

' "– enough to feed his family".' I nodded.

'Then, we want the vote. Aye,' he said, noting my surprise, 'we've had enough of yon pack of rich men and lords making our decisions for us. It's time we had a say in running the country, too.'

To me that sounded revolutionary enough, but I didn't say anything. ' "– all men have the vote." What's next?'

'And no more of this taking children into the mill, then throwing them out when they get older. If there must be children, let them be proper apprentices, trained into a proper job. That's what the law says: let it be enforced.'

'I thought children wanted to work,' I interrupted. 'Mr Moore tells me that he has too many children asking for a place in his factory: he has to turn them away.'

'Mr Moore—' He was about to spit, then remembered my presence. 'Lady, no child wants to work in the dust for twelve hours a day. They do it because they have to: because their fathers can't find work. And the reason their fathers can't find work is because the masters can get away with paying the children a third of a man's wage.'

' "– legally enforced system of apprenticeship",' I continued to write without saying another word. 'And then?'

'An end to the Combination Acts that stop workers getting together in a union to face their masters.'

'Is that illegal? It doesn't seem to have stopped you.'

'Aye, it's illegal. And you know who brought that law in? Bloody – sorry, lady, *blessed* William Wilberforce, that's who. Yorkshire's own Member of Parliament. He's done a grand job of fighting the slave trade, but he's done bugg– he's done nowt to help his own fellow Yorkshiremen: unless they have the vote, of course. Now you see why we want the vote ourselves.'

'I don't see why you should have the vote and not me,' I objected, starting to feel revolutionary myself.

'Fine, fine, put it in. Votes for women. It's got just as much chance as the rest of it. And let's have pigs with wings while we're about it.' He stopped, then shrugged his shoulders. 'I'm sorry. I can see tha's taken this to heart.'

' "– an end to the Combination Acts",' I continued inexorably.

'Ah well. They aren't to pass the Frame-breaking Act, of course. And an end to the Orders in Council. Since we're at it, let's put in summat for the Notts Ludds: no more shoddy work. That's cut-up stockings that sell for cheaper than well-fashioned ones, then fall to pieces,' he added in explanation.

'Aren't there Luddites in Lancashire? What do they want?'

'Oh, God knows,' he said with a true Yorkshireman's contempt for anything that came from across the Pennines. 'Forget them.'

'Anything else?'

'Nay, I think that's all.'

'Haven't you missed something? No more shearing-frames?'

He put his head back and laughed. 'Oh, aye, put that in.'

'Just let me finish this off and check it.' I did so, then offered it to him to sign. He took my pen: it was tiny in his hand, and he wrote awkwardly.

*General Ludd*

Sir Philip may write bad poetry, I thought, but at least he can write.

I folded the letter up. 'I'll make sure this gets delivered safely,' I said. 'Perhaps something will come of it.'

'If tha can get owt at all, then tha'll be a miracle worker,' he said, gloomily.

'Well, don't despair. And now I must go,' I said, moving towards the cart.

'Must tha?'

It was all he said – but the way he looked at me spoke far more. Far too much for my peace of mind.

'I – I—' I stopped, then shook myself mentally. 'Yes, I must. Goodbye, Mr Thomas Mellor of Robin Hood's Tower.'

'Goodbye, Miss Shirley Keeldar of Fieldhead. Until the next time.'

'Yes. Until the next time.'

'I wish you would not walk home alone after dark, Mr Moore,' I said as we finished that day's business and he prepared to go. 'You have made too many enemies. Let me drive you in the cart.'

'You have a poor opinion of me if you think that I need to shelter behind a woman's skirt. I always carry a brace of pistols, and Tartar is waiting for me.'

Tartar looked less than threatening: he was lying on his back in front of our roaring open fire, showing everything he had. Mrs Pryor knelt down beside him and scratched his belly. 'Now, Tartar, be a good, fierce dog and protect your master.' He slobbered ecstatically. I confess I held back: I was still afraid of dogs.

'Up, boy,' said Robert Moore as he put on his hat and opened the door. 'Good night, Miss Keeldar, Mrs Pryor,' he said and left, Tartar following to heel.

'I do hope that you'll overcome your fear of dogs,' said Mrs Pryor, while we were having a comfortable gossip before bed, 'now that you know that you're in no danger of hydrophobia.' She looked at me meaningfully.

'It's difficult to conceal anything from you,' I admitted. 'Yes, I've seen the man who was bitten with me, and he's alive and very healthy.'

'I hope you didn't fling your arms around him and kiss him passionately,' she said, joking.

'No, I restrained myself,' I managed to joke back. 'I should have told you, but—' I broke off.

'But it meant you would no longer have an excuse to defer your marriage?'

I nodded. 'I like Sir Philip very well, but I'm enjoying my freedom.'

'Is that how you feel about marriage? That it's some kind of prison? Yet Sir Philip is a good man who loves you dearly, and who would cherish you.'

'I know. But he writes such bad poetry!'

She laughed a little bitterly. 'There are worse vices in a husband than bad poetry, my dear. Cruelty. Infidelity. Drunkenness.'

I looked at her with some surprise. 'You speak as if you had some experience of those vices.' She said nothing. 'Very well. I shall not be impertinent enough to press you.' I'd always thought that she had a Past, and I wondered about Mr Pryor.

'You won't think me impertinent if I ask whether there's another man you'd prefer to marry?' She gave a slight glance at the door through which Robert Moore had just left.

That wasn't an idea I wished to encourage. 'There's no other man I'd even consider marrying.'

'I'm happy to hear it. But I'm even happier to know that you're safe from infection.' She embraced me. 'What are you going to do in November when your excuse for not marrying Sir Philip runs out?'

'Think about it in October.'

Suddenly we heard the sound of shouts and barking. There was a pistol-shot, then another. A human scream, then a canine yelp. I rushed to get my blunderbuss, and loaded it as I ran out towards the sound. There was very little moon, and I was upon them almost before I saw them.

Robert Moore was upright, obviously unharmed, looking about him. At his feet were two bodies: Tartar's, and that of a man, his face blackened with soot. The man was groaning: the dog was whimpering.

'There were two of them,' said Robert Moore. 'The other one got away, damn him.'

*Who was the other man?* I fretted for a moment. No, it couldn't have been him: he wouldn't have run away leaving his comrade, I was certain of that. There were plenty of other Luddites with a grudge against Robert Moore.

He knelt to look at the wounded man. 'He'll live. Miss Keeldar, would you be so good as to fetch your cart? We'll deliver him to the authorities.'

'Not the doctor?' I enquired mildly.

'He'll get the treatment he deserves. Leave me your blunderbuss.'

'What about Tartar?'

'It'd have gone badly for me if it wasn't for that dog. Bring him in your cart, too: we'll get him into the light and see what can be done.'

I ran back to Fieldhead and roused Johnnie, the man-of-all-work. He helped Robert Moore to load both man and dog into the cart, and we drove as fast as we could (which was not very fast over the bad road and with no light) to Briarfield, where we handed the wounded man over to the authorities.

At my insistence, a doctor was called. This proved to be Dr Kerr, who was obviously pleased to see me looking well.

'Let me have a look at you,' he said, drawing me into a private room despite my protests. 'You're much more important than a rascally Luddite. Hmm,' he said as he looked at my ankle. 'You'll have a scar there for the rest of your life, but it's healed very well. You said that there was someone else bitten with you? Have you seen him recently?'

'Yes, and he is extremely fit and healthy.'

'Then we may say that there is no further chance of infection. I am delighted to be able to tell you that you are perfectly safe. Now,' he said as we returned to the others, 'let me see to this villain. What's the matter with him?'

'Bullet-wound and dog-bite. But the dog's not mad: here he is to prove it.'

Dr Kerr was none too gentle with the wounded man, but he

was proficient. 'There, that'll have him safe for the hangman,' he said as he started to pack up.

'Before you go, Dr Kerr, would you – I know it's beneath your dignity, but could you possibly look at the dog as well?'

'Er—'

Robert Moore backed me up. 'I'd be most obliged, sir. The dog did save my life tonight.'

Dr Kerr nodded and felt Tartar's wounds, showing rather more gentleness than he had with the man. 'Well,' he said as he finished his inspection. 'He has a broken – shoulder, I suppose you would call it. If this were a man, I'd say that there's nothing the matter with him that good treatment and a month's rest wouldn't cure. But as it's a dog—'

Robert Moore thought for a second. 'Do you have anything in your bag that'll kill it painlessly?'

'What?' I was shocked. 'You heard the doctor say he can be treated!'

'Yes, and I heard him say it would be long and expensive. I can buy another dog for less.'

'But he saved your life! Have you no gratitude, no regard for loyal service?'

He looked at me coldly. 'I have no sentiment. No wish to spend time and money on a useless mouth.'

What a frightening man! An excellent clothier, no doubt – but what a dreadful husband he would make. 'Very well, I'll take him off your hands. Dr Kerr: please treat him, and I'll pay your fee.'

So Tartar came into my life, and I overcame my fear of dogs.

Tartar was a most chivalrous dog. He loved women: he hated men. Towards Robert Moore he showed a quite misplaced devotion, and he learned to tolerate Johnnie, whose work it became to feed him, but any other man received at best a muted growl, and at worst a ferocious bark.

He was muttering at Sir Philip, who had come to transport us to his house to prepare for the meeting, and I would have liked to growl too when Sir Philip said, 'Shirley, I have written a poem for the occasion. If the Luddites have their songs, should not we? Listen:

> *Welcome, welcome, Lord Lieutenant*
> *In your fight 'gainst General Ludd.*
> *We'll enlist behind your pennant,*
> *Grind their faces in the mud.*

What do you think?'

'Um . . .' I said, staring at the ceiling, not daring to catch Mrs Pryor's eye. 'I – er – I don't think so.'

'Oh,' he said dejectedly. 'What's wrong with it?'

Everything, I thought but didn't say. 'Well, for a start, *Ludd* doesn't rhyme with *mud*. It rhymes with *good*.'

'*Ludd*, *mud*, what's wrong with that?' he said, pronouncing the words to rhyme.

'It's *General Ludd*, like *Robin Hood*,' I replied, likewise suiting the pronunciation to the rhyme.

'I think,' said Mrs Pryor, ever the peacemaker, 'that it depends on whether you say the word with a northern or a southern accent.'

'And since the *Luddites*' – I pronounced it in the northern fashion – 'are all northerners, let us say it their way.' The argument would have gone on some time had not Caroline Helstone arrived, and we departed.

I know that Tom Mellor thought I was naïve, and you may agree with him, reader. But I was not that naïve. I did not imagine that I had only to say, 'Let's end poverty,' and everyone would applaud and say, 'What a good idea! Why didn't we think of that? Let's do it.'

No, my plans were of a different kind. My duty was to ensure that everyone was well-fed and happy, for well-fed and happy men are much more likely to talk peace than hungry, angry ones. Sir Philip had given me a free hand with the costs: this meeting would be important to him, as it would establish him in everyone else's eyes as he was in his own, the leading man of the district.

The Wednesday before Easter was, of course, still in the fasting period of Lent, and some sensibilities would be ruffled, especially in that year of poor harvests, by any display of profusion. To add to my difficulties, Easter was early that year and the weather was still wintry. So I planned on quality rather than quantity. A French chef had been hired at enormous cost, and southern forcing houses yielded up their expensive bounty to produce out-of-season fruit and vegetables. Extra servants had been taken on, and were busily polishing the silver and the chandeliers, dusting out the spare bedrooms, washing and drying curtains and coverlets (no easy task at that time of year) and, in general, making the house sparkle. Earl Fitzwilliam would have the main guest room, reputed to have been slept in by Queen Elizabeth (that woman seemed to have slept everywhere). Some of the lesser mortals would have to share rooms, as there were not enough to go round.

Captain Keeldar had bullied her lieutenants into letting her buy them new dresses for the occasion, and, when our party assembled on the evening before the meeting to greet the Lord Lieutenant, Mrs Pryor appeared in neat grey silk, and Caroline was looking very pretty in her (apparently simple but in fact very subtle) flowered muslin. I was, of course, in my beautiful peach-silk dress.

Earl Fitzwilliam was head of one of the aristocratic Whig families that had ruled England effortlessly in much of the last century, but languished in opposition in the new. He was in his sixties at the time of which I write, and, though he was not actually wearing the powder and satin of a previous era, looked as if he had only just put them off. I made my curtsy, and then looked up at the most cynical, shrewd and calculating eyes that I have ever seen.

But they were eyes which still appreciated pretty young women, and in a very short time he was sitting on the sofa with Caroline and myself on either side.

'Ah,' he said, leaning forward and picking up the book that was lying opened on the table: *Childe Harold's Pilgrimage*. 'I see that Byron-mania has reached even here.'

'We are not in the jungle, my lord,' I replied. 'That, surely, must be the only place that it has not reached in the past fortnight.' My cousin Henry, bless him, had sent me one of the first edition, and Caroline and I had been avid readers in our few spare moments.

'I had thought to escape foolish young women enthralled by this romantic tosh,' he said. 'But I see that I am forestalled, and will have to take second place in your hearts.'

'Surely *Earl* Fitzwilliam will not give precedence to a mere *Lord* Byron,' said Caroline: rather good, I thought, wishing I had said it myself. The flattery of an earl, even one old enough to be her grandfather, had charmed her into a delightful sparkle. A kind, lovable man he was not, but he was still doing a good job of putting Robert Moore out of her head.

'Alas, Miss Helstone, I fear I may have to,' he smiled. 'And not only in the hearts of delightful young ladies. If I may bring politics and Luddism into the conversation—'

'Of course you may,' I said. 'It is, after all, why we are here.'

'Did you read of young Byron's speech defending the Luddites against the Frame-breaking Bill?' Of course we had. 'You may then have picked up some glimmer of its brilliance. But I was there: I heard him. There has never been, in my entire career, a better maiden speech in either House of Parliament. I didn't agree with all of it, but he made me wish that I did. That young man has a first-rate career ahead of him in politics, so long as he doesn't have his head turned by this poetry nonsense.'

'I hope he stays with poetry, my lord,' I said. 'We have plenty of good politicians, but so very few good poets.' I wished I had a better one myself.

A few carefully selected people were invited to dinner, which was followed by a small dance which seemed impromptu but was the result of meticulous planning. I was alert, watching for hitches, but everything was going well. Earl Fitzwilliam claimed his privilege of dancing with the pretty girls, and Sir Philip accepted his duty of dancing with the plainer ones.

'May I ask for the honour of this dance?' came the voice of Robert Moore beside me.

'No, thank you, I do not dance tonight, Mr Moore. But Miss Helstone – oh, no, I see she has a partner already.' As if I had not already seen her prettily accepting the compliments of Earl Fitzwilliam as he showed what experience could do in his elegant, if stately, movements. But I wanted to ensure that Robert Moore had seen her, too. He had, and the phrase *dog in the manger* sprang to my mind. It was obviously doing him good to see her so beautiful, so courted, and so little in need of him.

Next day, love had to give way to politics. I was up early, to ensure I caught the post when it arrived. I diverted the footman's attention so I could slip General Ludd's letter in with the others on the tray, and followed him in to where Earl Fitzwilliam was conversing with half a dozen mill-owners and clothiers. Out of the corner of my eye as I ensured their needs were satisfied, I watched Earl Fitzwilliam pick up the letter and start to read it. He showed no reaction, but simply stuffed it in his pocket. He was going to keep it quiet!

*Oh, no you don't,* I thought, as I considered how to outflank him. I went up to Caroline and Mrs Pryor's room, and for about fifteen minutes we discussed preparations for the day. We gossiped a little about our visitors, and then I said, idly, 'Oh, and I gather that General Ludd has had the impertinence to send a letter to Earl Fitzwilliam himself!'

'How outrageous!' said Mrs Pryor.

'I wonder what was in it,' said Caroline.

'I doubt if anyone will see fit to tell us poor women,' said I.

That was all that was necessary. By mid-morning, every woman in the house had heard of General Ludd's letter, and, by the time the main meeting assembled at noon, so had all their husbands.

I was the only woman there. Not, of course, with the dignity of mill-owner, but Lady Nunnely was more than ready to give me the part of hostess, and I felt I could hover attentively, catering for those lords of creation, the men, without anyone plucking up the courage to object to my presence.

The matter of General Ludd's letter came up at once.

'I see that everyone has heard of it,' Earl Fitzwilliam said as he took it out of his pocket, 'so I shall read it to you.' I wished he hadn't shot such a glance in my direction. He couldn't have guessed that I had anything to do with it, could he?

As he read, the murmuring began: a low growl, mounting to the sound of thunder. When he finished, there was an uproar. 'Disgraceful!' 'Hang the fellow!' 'Treason!' were just some of the phrases I could distinguish. And I had used such conciliatory language, so desperate was I to be a peacemaker. All wasted, completely wasted!

Earl Fitzwilliam held up his hand, and the uproar died down. 'I think I have gathered your sentiments on that, gentlemen,' he said as he put the letter away. 'The only comment I would make in passing is that it is written in a vastly more literate – if somewhat effeminate – hand than has been General Ludd's habit in the past. It seems that educated men are joining the Luddites: a dangerous sign, I suggest.'

That was it. They took no further notice. Even when the discussion turned to the Orders in Council, and Earl Fitzwilliam agreed to carry their petition against it to Parliament, nobody commented that the Luddites wanted that too.

I watched them, the lords of creation, with increasing contempt. They were so full of sound and fury, so eager for blood, so lacking either compassion or courage. Oh, they could roar their approval at greater rewards for informers, at calls for more soldiers, at more and more hangings, so long as it did not involve their necks or their profits.

For when it came to the question of whether they would install the shearing frames, almost all of them backed off. Only Robert Moore and a few other clothiers dared to defy the Luddites and swear to have the frames, and to fight for them if need be.

And hardly a word was said about why so many poor men dared to defy the noose and take up the hammer, nor of why thousands more supported them and failed to inform against them. Mr Yorke, a radical clothier who'd refused to install the frames from conscience rather than cowardice, tried to raise the issue, but was shouted down.

Even some of the clergymen were bloodthirsty: Mr Helstone was as fiery as Robert Moore, though I noticed that Mr Hall, the kindly vicar of the next parish to Briarfield, was quietly distressed at the cries for blood.

Earl Fitzwilliam seemed mild in comparison. 'My duty is to stamp out Luddism,' he said at one point, 'not to persecute Luddites. If I must hang a dozen, or a hundred, or a thousand, I shall do so. But I shall hang no more than I must.' I watched in admiration of his skill as he forced through an agreement that it should be easy for a man to leave off his Luddism and to become 'untwisted'; to renounce, without penalty, without even being required to inform on his fellows, the fearful oath he had taken when he had been 'twisted in' and joined the Luddites.

The meeting was coming to a close, when, to my surprise and everyone else's, Earl Fitzwilliam turned towards me. 'We have not heard from the ladies yet. Miss Keeldar, you own a mill. What is your opinion?'

I was not prepared for this. Did he suspect I had anything to do with the letter, and was he offering me rope so I could hang myself? I know a lost cause when I see one, so I made no mention of the ideas in the letter. Perhaps, all the same, I could do something.

'My lord, gentlemen, I hope you will forgive a woman speaking to you. But charity has always been a woman's virtue, and perhaps it is my duty to bring it to your attention. The poor of Briarfield, of the whole of the West Riding. are badly off: some are starving to death. They must be helped. I know some say we should not give alms to the poor. For those who are not hungry, it's easy to palaver about the degradation of charity, but they forget the brevity of life as well as its bitterness. We none of us have long to live: let us help each other through seasons of want and woe as well as we can without heeding the scruples of vain philosophy.

'And not just for the sake of the poor, gentlemen, but for our own. If charity is too womanly a virtue, consider the manly one of prudence. I want to prevent mischief. I cannot forget, either day or night, that these embittered feelings of the poor against the rich have been generated in suffering: they would not be so bitter against us if they did not think us so much happier than themselves. Let us allay this suffering, and thereby lessen this bitterness. Let us, out of our abundance, give abundantly. Let us listen to Mercy before her voice is drowned by the shout of ruffian defiance. For if we do not, some day our brother's blood will be crying to Heaven against us.'

That went very well for a maiden speech, I thought, as I saw the nods of approval.

'Miss Keeldar, what do you suggest specifically?' asked Earl Fitzwilliam in a friendly tone.

'I suggest that, here and now, we appoint a committee to receive our money and to spend it to help our poor. If that is done, and if it is in the hands of men who are known for their charity and understanding of the poor as well as their prudence, I shall be the first to give; the committee shall have my note of hand for three hundred pounds.'

'I shall match your abundance with my own,' replied Earl Fitzwilliam promptly. 'I too shall give three hundred pounds.'

After that, of course, the money came pouring in. As I intended, Mr Hall, that kindly clergyman, was unanimously chosen to manage the fund, and the radical Mr Yorke was his second.

Then everyone went off to dinner. One or two looked a little guilty as they ate the expensive food in front of them, but they enjoyed it nevertheless.

When the gentlemen rejoined the ladies after dinner, Earl Fitzwilliam came straight to me.

'Miss Keeldar, may I offer you both my sincere congratulations and my thanks? This has been an excellent meeting, largely, I believe, due to your good offices. I achieved everything I wanted – but, of course, I usually do.'

'Thank you, my lord. May I in return offer my admiration of the way you handled it? I liked both your lack of desire for blood, and the way you persuaded the meeting that it was the wiser course as well as the more compassionate one.'

'Thank you. The admiration of a woman such as yourself is

worth having. But I fear that I must disillusion you; I am not so compassionate as you think.'

'You appeared so.'

'Let me tell you a fable that might make the point. Once upon a time, there was a man lying injured on a battlefield, flies buzzing round his wounds. Another man came and tried to wave away the flies. But the wounded man stopped him, saying, "Leave them alone. These flies have fed: they're not so hungry. But if you chase them away, they'll be replaced by new flies, and those will take a lot more blood". Miss Keeldar, I and my kind, the Whig aristocracy, we're the old flies. We've fed on the body of England and we are no longer hungry. But the men you saw this afternoon, the men of the nineteenth century – they're the new flies. They're greedy, and they're out for blood.'

I stared at him, revolted at such an open avowal, and scared at the thought that he might be right.

'I shock you with my cynicism,' he continued. 'Yet you have your share. You argued this afternoon that we must buy off the poor and dry up the sources of bitterness from which Luddism springs, that charity is not for their sake but for ours. That shows a certain cynicism, does it not? And to use your womanly weakness as a weapon: it was excellently done. You won't be offended if I say that yours was only the second best speech I've heard this year, for there is no disgrace in acknowledging Lord Byron as your superior. Indeed, I venture to say that yours was better than Byron's: not in eloquence, but in effect. For his speech could not prevent the passage of the Frame-breaking Bill, but yours has brought in three thousand pounds.'

'I am gratified by your approval, my lord.'

'Do I detect in you an ambition to become a political hostess?'

'It's not possible: Sir Philip is not interested in a seat in Parliament.'

He glanced at Sir Philip reading his poetry to three young

women, and sighed. I was vexed with Earl Fitzwilliam for sighing so ungraciously about his host; and I was vexed with his host for being so sighable about.

'Besides,' he continued, 'Sir Philip is a Tory, and though they might be in power, they give far worse dinners than we do. It's a waste, though. I think that you are a very clever woman.' There was more than flattery in his tone, so I looked enquiringly at him. He seemed to ignore my enquiry. 'To change the subject, I wonder how General Ludd's letter came to be common knowledge.'

'You know how servants will talk, my lord. I imagine the footman saw it when he brought it to you.'

'Hmm. It is a pity, perhaps, that the writer was not here in person. It would have been illuminating.'

'Oh, you should have told me: I would have invited him,' I said lightly.

'You are on such terms with him, of course,' he answered, equally lightly.

'Of course, my lord. I have had dealings with him. You have perhaps heard the story of how I failed to shoot him.'

'I have indeed. And may I say that it was very wise of you to fail: I think that neither you nor your party would have survived him long. They are dangerous men, the Luddites. I beseech you to be careful in any further dealings you have with them.'

'I think I'm safe. They don't make war on women: he told me so himself.'

'A most chivalrous gentleman.'

'He certainly was towards me.'

He took a pinch of snuff. 'Miss Keeldar,' he said, in a rather more earnest tone than before. 'Will you listen to some advice from someone who has seen very much more of the world than you?'

'Of course, my lord. I should be most grateful.' Listen to it, certainly. Take it, not necessarily.

'Well, then. It seems to me that you have – what shall I say? – a certain *interest* in this man.' He held up his hand to quell my instant protest. 'No, no, it is quite natural. There is always a charm in the outlaw, the rebel, the Robin Hood. See how all the foolish young women are enraptured by Byron's creation.'

'I am not a foolish young woman, my lord.'

'Not foolish, certainly. But you are a young woman. Do not be led into folly by romantic fancy.'

Romantic fancy? I thought as I climbed out of the cart. Surely not. He stood there, with his huge unromantic hands, and his rough unromantic clogs, and his worn unromantic clothes – this outlaw and rebel who met me at Robin Hood's Tower.

Perhaps Earl Fitzwilliam had a point.

'Didn't work, then?' He wasn't smiling, and I wished he would.

'No, no, how can you say that? There's a petition going to Parliament against the Orders in Council: that's one of the things you wanted. And there's three thousand pounds collected to help the poor.' Then I met his eyes, and slumped. 'No, it didn't work.'

'The grand speech you made about charity went down well amongst the clothiers.'

'How did you know that?' I asked in surprise.

'Don't be daft. With fifty servants working there?'

'Servants' talk, I suppose.'

'Aye, servants talk. And they talk about what matters to them, same as their betters.'

'But how can this matter to them? They aren't croppers. They aren't going to be put out of work by machines.'

'It matters to every poor man and woman in the West Riding.

It's not just about the frames. It's about being poor or being rich. You're rich, I'm poor,' he sighed bitterly. 'There's a gap between us as wide as the world.'

'It can't be bridged? By people coming together as friends, as you and I do?' I pleaded, conscious of the dreadful distance of his *you*, instead of the warm companionable *thee*.

'Friends?' he said in contemptuous disbelief. 'We're at *war*, lady. It's like an army of occupation in enemy territory. Because that's what you are, you rich. You hold us poor down by force. Most of the time you don't need soldiers: you have your mills and your bills. It's only times like these when you call your army in. Aye, and you're part of it, Miss Keeldar, you and the other charitable ones. And the cleverest part of it, too. You seek to buy us off: your grand speech told me that. But it's money you've stolen from us that you seek to do it with. And then you seek to charm us with your kindness and condescension. You speak of friendship, but it's a lie. There's no real friendship between you and me, and never can be.'

I was blinking and gulping as he spoke: I'd not show him my tears. This was cold, dyed-in-the-wool hostility, not the warm anger of our earlier argument, easy to quell with a smile and a handshake. We were enemies, and it was folly to think we could be something else.

I turned to leave. 'Very well, General Ludd. It's war,' I said, with barely a catch in my voice.

But then, in a voice much hoarser than my own, he cried out, 'Nay! Don't go like that!' He seized me and turned me round to face him again. 'I tried to drive thee away, but I can't do it.' A horny finger softly brushed away the single tear that I hadn't been able to keep back. 'God knows it hurt me to tell thee the truth. But I can see that I've hurt thee too, and I can't bear to.'

He held my shoulders in a grip that was as gentle as it was immovable. He was a cropper, a man whose livelihood depended on the strength and delicacy of his hands. And I was part of destroying that livelihood.

'It's not kindness and condescension that brings me here,' I said, putting my own hands up flat against his chest. To touch him, or to push him away from me? Both, I think. There were powerful forces attracting us, and powerful forces repelling us, and he was even more torn between them than I was.

'I were wrong about that. But I were right about the rest. Thee and me would be lying to ourselves and each other if we said we could be friends.'

'Very well, we'll lie. We can be friends; we can bridge the gap. I won't let the width of the world come between us. And you're not a man who submits to the world, are you?'

'Nay, I never have been, have I?' At last he gave me that wonderful smile again. 'But – friends?' he added doubtfully.

'Yes, friends.' Perhaps at that point we could find a secure balance between the forces that attracted and repelled.

'Right, friends it is, lady,' he said with determination. 'Damn the world! Let's lie.' As one, we let our hands fall from each other's bodies, and took up a stance more appropriate to friendship.

'And if we're to be friends,' I began, 'you can stop calling me *lady*. What's a lady? A female lord. A class enemy.'

'What shall I call thee?'

'What would you call me if I were poor?'

'Well, I'd call thee thy Christian name, or say *lass*, or – or *love*.'

'Go on, then, *lad*. Say it.'

'Well—'

'Coom on, Tom. Tha can do it,' I said in a vile imitation of his accent that made him laugh.

'I'd best teach thee to speak good Yorkshire, *lass*.'

'And the Christian name. Out with it.'

'Shirley. Aye, Shirley. See? I can say it.'

'I thank thee, friend Tom.'

'I thank thee, friend Shirley.'

It was a lie, and it was folly to think otherwise. But there are times when we need lies.

So began our month of friendship. It wasn't hard to keep up the lie for a while. Two people who like to be with each other can always find something to talk about and a joke to share. Every Friday we'd meet at Robin Hood's Tower at noon, then part an hour or so later. By unspoken agreement we stayed off the things that drove us apart: the frames, our politics, our very different lives and backgrounds. But that meant only that we searched for things that we had in common, and we found many. Our love of the Yorkshire Moors; our impatience with pomposity and respectability; our dislike of Mr Helstone (and I confess that I giggled in church the Sunday after Tom said, 'Now there's a man who looks like he's suffering a bad case of piles.')

I was happy and active in the rest of my life, but that brief meeting every Friday was the thing I always most looked forward to and looked back on. Perhaps it was the same for him: I don't know how happy he was the rest of the week, but he was certainly active – the Luddite attacks were reaching their peak that April. But for an hour or so each week, the mill-owner and the Luddite leader had an island of peace together, in the beautiful scenery of the moors in spring.

All the same, even the safest-seeming conversation could have an edge. One Friday we were talking about an obvious topic, given our meeting place: Robin Hood. We were united in common Yorkshire irritation at the way that Nottinghamshire had appropriated all the legends, when we knew that he'd breathed his last not a furlong from here. Then I mentioned that he'd been Earl of Huntingdon.

'Robin Hood an earl? Give over, lass. An earl robbing the rich to help the poor?'

'Of course he was an earl. Everyone knows that.' Then I thought about it. 'Oh. Everyone *I* know knows that.'

'Aye. And everyone *I* know, the people who don't own printing-houses and don't write books and can't afford news-papers, they know that Robin Hood was a poor man like them.' He grimaced. 'The rich! They don't just steal our land and our jobs: they even steal our heroes!' He smiled at me. 'I'm sorry, lass. I didn't mean thee. Tha's not one of them.'

I was, but we were both much happier if we forgot it.

An hour later I was forced to remember it. I returned to Fieldhead that afternoon to find Robert Moore waiting for me, Tartar showing his normal misplaced adoration of him.

'I've made my preparations, Miss Keeldar,' he said. 'The frames will be in place on Monday morning.' He explained his plans to get them in safely and work them undisturbed; he even had Mr Helstone's blessing for him and a handful of loyal men to work on Sunday to install them while the mill was empty. 'I hope I've reassured you that you won't throw good money after bad?'

'Indeed you have, Mr Moore.' I had no excuse to refuse to sign the paper that would give him his loan. Mr Pearson had drawn it up weeks ago, and it had been in a drawer unsigned ever since. Oh, how much I wished there was an excuse! But I'd given my word, and I couldn't go back on it.

*Robert Moore is right*, I told myself. *Tom Mellor is wrong. Don't let romantic fancy get in the way.* I signed the paper.

'Thank you,' he said as he pocketed it. 'You won't regret this.'

I regretted it already.

The following Monday, just after six in the morning, I could hear gunfire coming from Hollows Mill. I dressed quickly and ran out to the top of the hill from which I could look down into the valley where the mill was. Outside the gates were the crop-pers; I could see them waving their fists impotently at the soldiers who were preventing their entry. They had been taken by surprise and turned off without notice.

The other workers were filing in, and I realized that I wasn't the only one with divided feelings. I knew that the frames were preserving their jobs; Tom Mellor knew that they supported his fight; and they knew that they had to go into the mill that day, or they'd be turned off too and they'd starve.

On the other side of the valley a man was running down the hill towards the croppers at the mill gates. He was a long way off, but I recognized him at once. He saw me: I must have been conspicuous on that green hill, for I was wearing a bright red dress, chosen because it was easy to put on in a hurry. He carried on running to join his comrades, but as he did so he gave me a friendly wave.

I waved back across the valley to him, conscious of the irony. Friendship wasn't going to bridge this gap.


'Eh up, lass,' he greeted me as I arrived at Robin Hood's Tower. 'That were a right colourful dress that tha wore on Monday.' So we could talk about my taste in fashion, or we could talk about the frames.

'Is it a good idea to mention what happened on Monday?'

'If Robert Moore puts frames in and turns the croppers off, it's nowt to do with thee. Tha's nobbut his landlord.'

I had to undeceive him: the lie of our friendship could stretch only so far.

'It does have something to do with me,' I said, resigning myself to the inevitable. 'I like you far too well to keep this from you. It was my money that Robert Moore used to buy the frames.'

He turned away from me and stared at the top of the tower

for a while in silence. 'It's a mite hard to keep on lying to ourselves after that,' he sighed.

'It is, isn't it?' I clambered into the cart, and he came and stood beside me.

'Enemies it must be then.' He took my hand. 'But it were grand that we were friends.'

'I'm glad we were. And perhaps we shall be again, when all this is over.'

'Aye. I'd like that. I thank thee for telling me the truth, though it's been a good lie.' Then his eyes twinkled. 'Just think! I've been lying with a mill-owner!'

'Tom!' I protested, half furious, half laughing. As I drove away, I heard his rich deep chuckle behind me. It had been a good lie, for at least now I could hope that perhaps one day I'd hear him laugh again.

# PART 4

It was the first of May. A generation before, the village lads and lasses would have been out celebrating May Day. But today their sons and daughters worked in mills that could not stop for merrymaking.

England was at war: not only with the French, but with itself. Hundreds of frames had been broken, mills had been attacked, men had been killed. Soldiers were billeted in every village; there were almost as many in the North fighting Englishmen as there were in the Peninsula fighting Frenchmen.

Three thousand pounds had saved many people from starving, but it had done nothing to stem the Luddite tide. Kindly Mr Hall and radical Mr Yorke had worked as hard, and as ineffectively, as I had to make peace. We had tried our best, and it wasn't enough.

I knew that Hollows Mill, my property, was going to come under attack: and I knew that leading the attack would be Tom Mellor. I could have prevented it. Yes, I could – if I had broken my word to Robert Moore and refused him the loan that he'd counted on. Or if I'd betrayed Tom and handed him over to the authorities. *Blessed are the peacemakers: for they shall be called the children of God* seemed bitterly ironic to me: I wasn't ruthless enough to be a peacemaker.

I was visiting Caroline at the Rectory and was just about to leave, when Mr Helstone stopped me. 'Would you care to stay here tonight, Miss Keeldar? I have an appointment elsewhere, and perhaps you would be so good as to keep my niece company.'

'And Mrs Pryor?'

'I'll send a message to Fieldhead to tell her where you are.'

A brace of pistols bulged unclerically under his coat: I could guess where his appointment was. Neither of us wanted to alarm Caroline so he accepted my slight nod towards the front gate, out of her hearing.

'In short, Mr Helstone, you want Captain Keeldar to guard your property, while you are off to guard hers.'

'Not just my property: my niece.'

'The attack will come tonight, then?'

'So Moore believes. Don't worry, Captain Keeldar. Moore is well prepared and fortified. He has soldiers a-plenty there as well as a few loyal men, and if the rascals succeed in breaking in, they'll find a very warm welcome. He has spiked rollers at the top of the stairs, and carboys of vitriol ready to pour down on them.'

'Oh, excellent!' I managed to say. 'Wonderful.'

'There's a brace of pistols over the mantelpiece in my study, loaded but not cocked. I'd not trust any other woman with them, but you're not one of the awkward squad.'

I watched him walk down the road towards Hollows Mill. Did I wish to go with him, or was I very glad of a reason not to?

Caroline and I ate our supper, sewed, and gossiped in French as we had often done before. But she was no fool: she knew something was in the air, and she wanted to go to bed no more than I did.

Towards midnight we were looking out of the window at the clear May stars when we heard it: the tramp of hundreds of feet coming down the road. Some of them stopped outside the Rectory, and we heard voices outside the garden wall, though we could not distinguish what they said.

This was intolerable. A pistol in each hand, I crept quietly down the path towards them: Caroline silently followed me. We breathed in the smell of the lilacs as we listened.

'If the damned parson fell out of a window and broke his neck, I'd be as glad as you would,' came a voice I knew very well. 'But he's not our main objective.'

'Leave me behind, then, and I'll settle him.'

'Oh, aye? And the womenfolk?'

'I'd let them alone – unless they shrieked.'

'And Parson Helstone keeps no weapons, I suppose?' said the voice with withering scorn.

'Aye. But—'

'Don't be a bloody fool, then. One shot and the militia would be on us. Come on, lads. Let's keep moving.'

The tramp of feet moved away down the road, and I sagged in relief. I could have defended us women against one man, but not the many that might have followed him. Tom Mellor didn't know it, but he had saved me again.

'Caroline, let's go. We can take a short cut over the fields and get there ahead of them.'

We locked up behind us and ran through the fields. The briars tore our dresses and the mud slowed our feet. Caroline was lagging behind me, and soon paused for a rest.

'Shirley, why are we doing this?' she panted.

'To give a warning, of course.'

'To whom?'

A good question. The men who were defending my property, or the man who was leading the attack? But there was only one answer that Caroline would acknowledge. 'To Robert Moore.'

At that she recovered her breath, and for a good five minutes ran ahead of me. But we were not fast enough. A shot blasted the air ahead of us, making us jump.

'No need for a warning, then. I think they know.'

Was there anything that I could do, even now, to stop it? Fling myself dramatically in between two groups of men at war and appeal to their chivalry? That would be as much use as my letter from General Ludd to Earl Fitzwilliam, as well as being highly embarrassing to all concerned.

We stood at the top of the hill, looking down on to the mill. There was almost no moon and all the lamps were out in the mill, but the stars were bright in the cloudless sky and our eyes were used to the darkness. We could see what appeared to be hundreds of shapes moving outside the mill wall: we could hear the sound of their hammers against the gates.

A crash.

'Shirley, the gates are down!' Caroline cried, starting down the hill. 'I must go to him!'

'Don't be a fool,' I said, catching her arm and stopping her flight. 'He doesn't want you there.'

'But I can help him!'

'What, by inspiring him into action?' I sneered. 'No man wants a woman in this. It isn't a tournament with knights in armour; it's about *money*. Robert's defending his balance sheet, and To – and the Luddites are defending their jobs. No, Caroline, all we can do is watch.'

You may think, reader, that I was talking to myself as much as Caroline. But that would not be entirely true. I don't think I could have moved: my feelings were so completely divided they immobilized me.

The Luddites marched through the gates with a discipline and courage worthy of a better cause. We could hear their dreadful shouts, full of hate: 'Murder them!' 'Burn it down!', 'Aye, and with the buggers in it!' There was no response from inside the mill. It seemed empty: it looked empty.

A silence fell over the attackers: what were they doing? Then, at one man's shout (and I knew whose it was) a shower of stones was hurled through the windows, and we heard the glass smash.

As if that were the signal for the defenders, a volley of gunfire crashed out. There were shrieks of pain from the attackers, and a howl of oaths. I could see them spread out: some were hammering at the mill doors, and a few were returning the fire from their muskets.

It was an even battle: there were many more of the attackers, but the defenders were far better armed, and were protected by the mill walls. The Luddite musket men were getting the worst of it: the defenders could pick them out from the flashes of their guns, and man after man cried out as he was hit.

I could just make out the silent shapes of men creeping round for an assault at the back of the mill while the defenders concentrated on the front. But if I could make them out, so could the single guard posted there. I heard him calling for help from his fellows in the mill, and soon the guns were firing at the back as well as the front.

There was a splash: someone must have fallen into the river that powered the mill wheel. *'Damn!'* I recognized the voice that cursed. There was another splash: had he dived in to rescue his comrade? It was the sort of thing he'd do. I gnawed my knuckles, knowing how strong and deadly was the current of the mill race. I strained to catch any sound that would tell me that he was safe. But I could hear nothing over the cries of defenders and attackers, and the musket shots, and the hammering.

The shots from the Luddites ceased; they had run out of ammunition, or of men to fire it.

A shout. 'It's no use, lads. Retreat!' It was his voice, and I felt almost sick with relief for him. And relief that my mill had been saved from him and his lads. And relief that there had been no use for spiked rollers and vitriol.

There was no cessation of the barrage from the muskets inside the mill as we saw the men stream back out of the gates. But outside the walls they were safe: the firing from the mill ceased, and we could hear the Luddites being numbered off, and we heard how many men did not answer to their numbers – the wounded, still inside the gates, who would hang if they survived their injuries.

Dawn was just beginning, and with its light we saw some twenty men creep back inside the gates and move towards the wounded. But the men inside the mill must have seen them too and opened fire again. It seemed incredible that those who were trying to carry off their wounded were not all killed, but they kept on: one by one the wounded were picked up and carried out.

There were half a dozen bodies left in the mill yard, close to the mill itself and difficult to rescue. I saw one man – at that distance I don't know how I recognized him, but I did – run towards one of the bodies by the mill wall. He bent to lift his comrade: there was a crash of muskets, and he fell.

A howl of dismay came from the Luddites who were watching from outside the gates – a howl which I wanted to echo – and then they fled.

It was over, and the rising sun revealed the sorry story. Barely a window was left in the mill, stones and bricks littered the yard, and crimson stained its earth.

'I must go to him now!' I heard Caroline beside me. I started: I had almost forgotten her presence.

'No,' I said, gripping her arm. 'He will not want you even now. He has had his triumph: he has won. Be content with that.'

She struggled: and an idea began to form in my mind. 'Do you really want to be useful to him?'

'More than anything in the world.'

110

'Then you can stop him having any more corpses on his hands than he must have. There are half a dozen wounded or dead men down there, and maybe more inside the mill. We can't do anything for the dead, but the wounded will be better cared for at Fieldhead than at the mill. So you run up to Fieldhead as fast as you can: they can't have slept through that noise. Tell Mrs Gill that she's to make up beds in the hall down-stairs for the wounded men, and get dressings and clean water ready. Then fetch Mrs Pryor in the cart. Put plenty of bedding-straw and blankets in it, so we can carry the wounded back up to Fieldhead. Bring some dressings as well; we'll bandage them before we try to move them. Oh, one more thing: bring plenty of beef and beer and bread; we'll give the soldiers a feast for what they've done.'

She turned without a word and ran up the hill towards Fieldhead. I walked, as composedly as I could manage, down the hill to the mill.

Robert Moore and his fellows were standing, tired, begrimed but triumphant, in the mill yard as I arrived. One of them was pumping water out for his thirsty colleagues.

'I have ordered a better reward for you than plain water,' I said. 'I thank you, Mr Moore, and I congratulate you. I thank you all!' I cried. 'You fought so well and bravely.' I was sincere: they had defended my property magnificently.

'You saw, then?' said Robert Moore.

'Yes, I was watching from the hill top.' I did not reveal Caroline's presence: if she wanted to tell him, she could. 'I have rarely seen anything braver.' I looked around the yard. 'Or anything more depressing than this.' The smashed glass: the smashed bodies. 'I wanted to prevent this.' Even if there had been no Tom Mellor in the case, I would not have wanted my property to cost the lives of so many men. Even the ones who were just wounded – and their groans told me that there were some – would live only long enough to face the hangman.

But there was a Tom Mellor in the case. The first thing I had to do was to find out if he was still alive; if he was, it would need a very cool head, free from all distractions of emotion and sentiment, to keep him that way.

'Look at them,' I said, my voice filled with scorn as I gestured to the bodies clustered by the mill door. 'What did they think they were doing, with their stones and hammers against armed and resolute men?' I walked over to them. 'With their faces begrimed with soot or covered in masks so no one would recognize them?' I pointed at one of them. 'We can recognize them now!'

A pair of bright blue eyes looked at me from over his mask. He was alive and conscious.

I forced down the surge of relief I felt; this was no time for me to show emotion. If I were to save him, he must play his part.

'Poor, pathetic, play-acting fools. Do you hear me, you?' I bent down and looked steadily at him, willing him to understand and trust me. 'Play-acting fools!'

One of the blue eyes closed in a slow wink. He understood me: play-acting fools everyone if it's done well.

I stood up. 'With your permission, I'll help save these vermin for the noose,' I said, gesturing to the bodies around me. 'I'll have these half-dozen men brought up to Fieldhead; the doctor – and the magistrate – can see them thére. Are any of our men hurt?'

'No, not a one.'

'Thank God for that. Ah, here's the cart already, with the refreshment that you deserve.' Johnnie drove it in, Mrs Pryor and Caroline squeezed beside him.

'Not for this one,' said Robert Moore, gesturing to one of the soldiers who stood apart from the rest. 'The coward refused to shoot. He'll get a hundred lashes for this, I swear!'

'Very well, sir,' I said to the soldier sternly. 'While your fellows are feasting on good beef and ale, you shall be on punishment duty.' My voice was as harsh as I could make it, to disguise the fact that inwardly I was rejoicing: he would make my plan a lot easier than I had expected.

There was no shortage of hands to unload the cart, and all the men were soon feasting, while Mrs Pryor and I helped Mr Helstone with immediate aid for the wounded.

'Johnnie, and you, sir,' to the recalcitrant soldier, 'will you load these half-dozen on to the cart? Start with this one,' I said, pointing to the masked man at my feet. 'Hey, carefully now! We want to save them for the hangman!'

I made sure he was stowed safely and securely at the end of the cart nearest the horses. 'Come on, now. Load the rest on.'

There were six more men lying in the yard. Johnnie called out as he kneeled over one of them. 'This one's dead, ma'am.'

'Well, load him on with the rest,' I said; another piece of my plan fell into place. 'Though you need not be so careful about him, of course.'

Johnnie and the soldier were loading the last of the wounded on to the cart when I turned to Mrs Pryor and said, 'Will you take Caroline back to the Rectory and stay with her? All night, if she needs you. She looks exhausted.'

Mrs Pryor rushed to Caroline. 'How are you, my dear? In truth, you don't look well. Come with me. Here, lean on my arm,' she said as she escorted Caroline through the gate.

That got rid of two of them. Now another.

'Johnnie, stay behind here and help Mr Moore clear up. But have your share of the feast. You' – I said to the soldier – 'you come with me back to Fieldhead, and help me at the other end.'

'Will you be safe, Miss Keeldar?' asked Robert Moore. 'Those are dangerous men, and that soldier is not to be trusted.'

'This soldier will do exactly what he's told.' Or so I very

much hoped. 'And Captain Keeldar has nothing to fear from these half-dozen wounded men,' I said. There would be *half a dozen wounded men* loaded on to the cart at this end: there would be *half a dozen Luddites* loaded off at the other. I hoped that confusion, stupidity and poor communication would cover the difference between those two phrases. After all, confusion, stupidity and poor communication are some of the most reliable features of human conduct.

But I had to change my plan; there was no chance for a wounded man to slip out of the cart and simply run off, for I could not prevent an armed guardsman riding with us as we drove off to Fieldhead. I'd have to try something more subtle.

From the men in cart behind us we could hear the occasional groan, and I drove as carefully and as smoothly as I could.

'You'd better ride ahead of us,' I said to the guard on horseback. 'Make sure that the road is clear.'

He went far enough ahead not to hear me as I spoke quietly to the soldier beside me in the cart. 'Bristow, isn't it?'

'Yes, ma'am.'

'The man who led off half our soldiers on a wild-goose chase last February as we were going over Stilborough Moor with the frames, and left the rest of us vulnerable to attack?'

'I'm sorry about that, ma'am. I didn't mean—'

I interrupted him. 'I wonder if Mr Moore has recognized you.'

'No, he hasn't, ma'am.'

'It'd be more than a hundred lashes if he did, you know.'

'Ma'am?' he said, thoroughly frightened now.

'Well, I don't suppose he will. So long as you do exactly as I say.'

'Of course, ma'am. Exactly as you say.'

There was a pause in the conversation as I negotiated a muddy puddle.

'You should be ashamed of yourself, Bristow, not looking after these men for the hangman,' I said when I could see that the mounted guard wasn't looking back at us. 'This one, for instance.' I reached behind me and touched the man closest to me: his hand gripped mine, then released it. 'His clothes are damp, and he's getting very cold. Find a blanket and cover him up.' The man in the cart huddled himself into a ball. 'Right up, now. Yes, cover his head: you can lose a lot of heat from your head, you know. My word, doesn't he look just like a pile of old sacking?'

Bristow gave me a very puzzled look. But one of the Luddites in the cart was conscious enough to know what was happening, and thought quickly enough not to be puzzled: he manoeuvred the corpse so that there were still six heads appearing over the top of the cart. I recognized him: William Brook, one of the croppers who'd been turned off from Hollows Mill.

I drove up to Fieldhead and summoned all the servants. Tartar was barking furiously, showing his usual dislike of men, even wounded ones. I'd forgotten about Tartar.

'Right,' I said to the servants and the mounted guard who'd accompanied us. 'I want these half-dozen men' – blessedly vague phrase, *half-dozen*, that could at a pinch mean anywhere from five to seven – 'carried carefully into the hall and looked after. None of you slacking off, now. Stay with them and look after them. You can get everything you need from the downstairs parlour. I'll just drive the cart round the back.'

Bristow wasn't puzzled any more. 'Yes,' he said to the servants and the other guard as he directed them in carrying off the wounded. 'These half-dozen men are to be handed over to the magistrate as soon as they're fit.'

'Oh, Mrs Gill: can you take Tartar and lock him in the shed? We can't have him disturbing these men, and the doctor will arrive very soon.'

William Brook, the last of the six to be taken off the cart, groaned and collapsed dramatically, attracting the attention of the servants who were still outside. They carried him, moaning enthusiastically, into the hall.

'Bristow,' I said quietly as I drove round the back. 'Do you see that small back door?'

'Yes, ma'am,' he said, grinning.

'Well, through that door is a small flight of stairs. And straight ahead of you at the top of the stairs there's a door into a room. If you go through that, you'll come to another room, with a bed in it: the second room, remember: it's mine.'

'Yes, ma'am.'

'Do you think you could carry this pile of old sacking up those stairs, through the first room, and into my bedroom without anyone noticing? We wouldn't want to disturb any of the servants, would we? They're all so busy looking after the wounded in the hall.'

'I think I could, ma'am.'

'And do you think you could carefully put this pile of old sacking on the bed, then bolt the door? And then stay with it, and look after it, and make sure nobody comes in until I get there?'

'Very good, ma'am,' he said as he lifted the – pile of old sacking – gently out of the cart. The pile of old sacking produced a pair of legs that could stagger, and an arm that went round Bristow's shoulder. They disappeared through the back door, and I went round to the front.

Yes, good. All the servants were in the hall, looking after the wounded men. One body was unattended: no attention could do him any good now. I knelt over him. There was a huge wound in his stomach: I could see his bowels. I took a cloth and washed the soot off his face – his young, unlined, dead face. I said a small prayer for him as I closed his eyes.

I went to William Brook and began to tend his wound. He was no longer groaning.

'All quiet now?' I asked.

'Aye, I can keep quiet,' he said. I hoped he could.

Dr Kerr arrived. He was no friend to the Luddites, but he was professional, and started work immediately 'I thought there were seven of them,' he said as he efficiently, if ruthlessly, pulled a bullet from a thigh, ignoring the cries of pain.

'No, six,' I shouted over the man's cries.

'Seven, I was told.'

'Six, that's right, isn't it, Mrs Gill?'

'Aye,' she said. 'There's the dead man, of course. Happen he were counted twice.'

Bless you, Mrs Gill, I thought. Carry on stealing my candles and my sugar as long as you like.

Mr Helstone arrived with some militia men. 'Where's the other one?'

'What other one?' said Dr Kerr.

'There were seven of them.'

'No, six. You counted the dead one twice.'

Mr Helstone looked puzzled for a moment, then shrugged and accepted the doctor's authority. I could leave them safely to it, now. Everyone firmly believed that the dead man had been counted twice.

'If you'll excuse me, gentlemen, I'll go to bed to catch up with my sleep. I feel soooo tired,' I yawned. 'Mr Helstone, Dr Kerr: my house and my servants are at your disposal. Just don't disturb me.'

I discreetly took a handful of dressings and a wet cloth, and went up the back stairs carefully erasing all the drops of blood. 'Bristow, it's me,' I whispered at my bedroom door. 'Miss Keeldar.'

He opened the door quietly and let me in. 'He's still

breathing, ma'am,' he whispered, 'but he's out cold.'

I went over to the bed, and looked at him: the wounded Luddite who'd led the attack on my property. He'd been knocked out by a bullet that – thank God – had only grazed his skull when he'd bent to lift his fallen comrade, and there was a shoulder wound as well. He'd lost blood: much of it over my best coverlet, I noticed. Bristow and I took off his mask, stripped off his jacket and shirt, washed the wounds to his head and shoulder, and bandaged him. He recovered enough consciousness to know what we were doing, but he went out again once we laid him back on the bed.

'You know not to breathe a word of this, don't you, Bristow?' I said quietly.

'Oh, yes, ma'am. It'd be my neck. And his. And yours.'

'Go downstairs and join the others now. I'll see what I can do to get the number of lashes brought down. I have some authority: it's my mill, after all.'

'I know, ma'am. So why—?'

'I could as well ask why you're in the militia and yet you help the Luddites.'

'It's him,' and I presumed he meant the man on the bed. 'He talked to me. Made me see what was right.'

'He saved my life once,' I said. 'I believe in paying my debts.'

That answer seemed to satisfy Bristow, and he left; as I bolted the door behind him I wished that it satisfied me.

I bundled up the bloodied clothing and bandages, then went to sit beside him on the bed, busying myself with thinking up an excuse for the washerwoman. There was not much else I could do, other than watch, try to keep my eyes open (I had not been lying when I said I was exhausted) and wait for that strong body to heal itself.

It *was* a strong body. I could see it, now his torso was bare, and I admitted to myself that I wanted to stroke it: the wide chest moving up and down as he breathed steadily, the great, sinewy muscles in his arms, the smooth round curve of his shoulder.

His face was relaxed in oblivion. Not a handsome face: I never thought it that. There was stubble on his jaw, and lines of strain that had not been there when I first saw him in the smithy, half a year ago. His lips were parted, and I contemplated them as I examined my emotions as unemotionally as I could.

Shall I kiss him? I asked myself. I could do it now, while he was unconscious: I could lean over that mighty body, and put my arms round him, and touch my lips to his – and nobody would ever know that I'd done it, not even he. I did not, but I had to work hard on my resolution, and remind myself of what he was and what I was, and bite my own lips as if to punish them for my desire to put them to such a use.

I felt his trousers – I had an excuse to do that. They were still slightly damp, but care for a patient could go too far, and I'd leave them on. Did he have to be so brave in a bad cause? As I'd guessed, he'd dived into the river near the mill race to rescue one of his lads, in the same way as he'd rushed into the fire of the muskets to rescue another.

In the same way as he'd been bitten by a mad dog to rescue a stranger.

My eyes kept closing, and I had to keep forcing them open. There was just enough space on the bed for me to lie down beside him. And rest. But I must not. I shook my head trying to keep myself awake. The bed looked so tempting. So very tempting. Very . . . very . . . very. . . .

I woke to find bright blue eyes looking at me.

'I'm dead and gone to Heaven,' he said, smiling broadly. 'I always knew I'd led a virtuous life.'

I jumped off the bed, blushing furiously at my impropriety. 'I must go downstairs to see what's happening,' I whispered. 'This door doesn't lock from the outside. Are you fit enough to get up and bolt it behind me?'

He winced in pain as he got up, but he managed to stand up, even if he did sway slightly. 'Aye, I'm right.' He was bare-footed – his clogs were lost somewhere between here and the mill – and he stepped quietly to the door and leaned against it. 'How many of them are down there, my lads?'

'Six. One dead. Another likely to be before the day's out.'

The pain of it clearly hurt him more than his wounds.

'Is there owt I can do to save the rest of them?'

'No. You'd only put your own head in the noose. And perhaps mine.'

'We failed, didn't we? *I* failed.'

'Yes.' There wasn't much else I could say, so I left him.

I'd come out of it fairly well, I reflected. He was safe: my mill was safe, though both were damaged. Which was the more important to me? I dared not even think about that.

Downstairs, four of the Luddites were well enough to be sitting up, with soldiers guarding them. I ordered Mrs Gill to provide tea and bread for everyone, and then I joined Mr Helstone and Dr Kerr round the fifth Luddite. It needed no doctor to tell me he was dying. He had a gaping wound in his chest, the ribs were smashed, and bright red blood was still pumping out of him.

Mr Helstone leaned over him. 'Young man, very soon you will face your Maker,' he said. 'You are dying, with your sins upon your soul. This is your last chance to confess, to cleanse yourself from sin.'

The man groaned, but said nothing.

'Confess your sins, young man. Make your soul as white as snow, and tell me the names of your comrades.'

With the last of his strength, the man lifted his head. 'Can you keep a secret?' he whispered.

'Yes, yes,' said Mr Helstone eagerly.

'So can I,' he gasped, and died.

The house was mine. I'd given all the servants the rest of the day off, and the night; it was Saturday, and there was a fair in the village to celebrate the May. Nothing like the old days, but enough to make my action seem nothing more than that of a generous employer. I sent with them a message to Mrs Pryor, telling her to keep Caroline company all night. The living Luddites had left with their guards; the dead ones had left with Mr Helstone and Dr Kerr. The former was refusing to give them Christian burial, and the latter was arguing that it was his duty to do so.

I went to the shed and unlocked Tartar: he greeted me enthusiastically, showing no resentment for his imprisonment. He accompanied me as I walked round the house: my house, with no servants, no Mrs Pryor, no visitors. I was alone, except for – I tried to think of him as an injured patient who needed nursing, but he was also a half-naked man in my bedroom, with a magnificent body, and bright blue eyes, and a smile that always warmed my heart.

I inspected places that I'd never normally enter: the kitchen, the stable, the servants' quarters. This was a drab little room, chill even in May with no place for a fire, in which all four of them slept. I was ashamed of myself.

I ran out of excuses, and I went to my own door. Tartar was with me: I was almost sure that I didn't need a dog's protection against the powerful man in my bedroom, but I was glad of it to cover the distance between *almost* and *completely*.

I knocked.

'It's me. It's all right – we're alone in the house.'

I heard the sound of him unbolting the door.

'Don't open it,' I said. 'Get back into bed. I've got a dog with me. He hates men, but perhaps he won't bark at you so much if you're lying down.'

I heard him move away from the door, and I opened it. Tartar bounded in, rushed over to him – and started licking his hands, tail wagging dementedly.

'Good old dog,' he said as he sat on the bed patting Tartar with a force that drove the dog to even more ecstatic behaviour. 'Dost tha want thy back scratched? There, now. Isn't that good?'

'How did you do that?' I asked, astonished. 'Tartar would have savaged any other man.'

'He were Moore's old guard dog, right?'

'Yes, and trained to kill.'

'Aye, I know the man who trained him. Trains all the guard dogs in these parts. I often visit him.' He was smiling broadly.

'Oh, and you just happen to make friends with all his dogs before he sells them, I suppose?'

'Aye. I like dogs, see?'

'I told you before, sir. You're a rogue.'

'I am that.' He lay back down on the bed, looking up at me. He wasn't smiling. 'We're even now, thee and me, I saved thy life: tha's saved mine. Tha's got no more obligation to me now. Tha's paid thy debt.'

'Oh, who talks of obligations and debts between friends?'

'Nay, not friends. Let's not lie to ourselves again.' His eyes were full of meaning. 'Enemies, aye. And happen – summat else.'

There was a long silence.

I don't want this, I thought. Not yet. Perhaps not ever.

'I see it this way,' I replied eventually. 'We're alone in this house together, until it gets dark and you can leave safely. Let's keep up the lie, at least for the rest of the day. Please?'

He turned his face away from me. 'Aye,' he said after a moment, still not looking at me. 'Happen tha's in the right – friend Shirley.'

'I am in the right – friend Tom.' I bustled round busily, to give us both time to put on faces of friendship. 'Is there anyone who'll treat that wound without informing on you? No, I don't want to know the name, but I think you still have the shot in you, and it wants taking out.'

'Aye, there is.'

'There's something else. At least two people – Bristow and William Brook – know that I helped you. You must make sure they keep quiet about it, even – especially – from the rest of your men. Tell Brook what I told Bristow, that I saved your life because you'd saved mine: it's a good reason. Make them understand that I'm no Luddite sympathizer: if any Luddites arrive on my doorstep and expect me to help them, they'll get a very unpleasant shock.'

'Bristow won't talk. And Bill – I'll trust thee enough to tell thee that it were his son that tha didn't shoot on Stilborough Moor. Gave the lad a right earful for not keeping his eye on thee, but he's grateful to thee.'

With that the Luddites ceased to be violent masked men in my mind, and became fathers and husbands.

'Are you tired?' I asked. 'You should rest, you know.'

'I'm hungry more than tired,' he said, sitting up.

'Good heavens, what a poor hostess you must think me! Of course you are. It's hungry work, trying to destroy other people's property.'

'Nay, love, that's not fair. That's talking like an enemy. Of course, if tha wants to stop being friends. . . .' His face expressed hunger for more than food, he was smiling that wonderful smile, and his blue eyes were laughing.

'Now you stay right there, friend Tom, and I'll be back in a moment. And if you keep on looking at me like that, it'll be nothing better than thin gruel!'

I was not so unfamiliar with my own kitchen that I couldn't find bread, cheese and beer. I took a tray up to my room, and we sat companionably eating and drinking together, for I was hungry too.

I searched for a safe topic of conversation. 'Don't tell me if you don't want to, but why *Ludd*? It's such a funny name. You say there are many of you General Ludds, but someone must have been the first one.'

He started to laugh, then choked on a mouthful of bread and cheese. 'Sorry, lass. Aye, there were an original Ned Ludd,' he chuckled.

'Stop laughing at me! If you don't want to say, don't, but otherwise tell me the joke.'

'Aye, that's exactly what it is, a joke. He lived down Notts way about thirty year back. He were a few ha'pence short of a shilling, and he couldn't touch owt without breaking it, and he had a right temper, so he broke a frame on purpose when it didn't do what he wanted. And so, when summat were broken and nobody knew who did it, folk'd say, "Ah, it must be Ned Ludd". And that's what they said to the magistrates when they first started breaking the frames.'

'So all this *General Ludd, hero of Nottinghamshire* business is a joke?'

'Aye. Anyone can write a letter and sign himself as General Ludd. I'm nobbut the man that the lads have chosen to do it round these parts.'

'Nobody special?'

'Nay, nobody special. Do I disappoint thee, love? Did tha think I were the hero of the West Riding?'

'I still think it. And I saw the way you led your men last night, and they think it, too.'

'That's nobbut a few things I picked up in the army.'

'You were a soldier! Of course: that explains the military discipline. But I thought you were a cropper.'

'Aye, I were, about four, five year ago. Until the frames put me out of work. I could have found another job – I'm a good cropper. But I thought I'd like to see summat outside the West Riding, so I joined up.'

'Which regiment? The Fifty-first?' Our local light infantry was famed for its courage and initiative.

'Aye. In the Peninsula.' His face became angry. 'That's one of the lies they tell against us Ludds: they say we're in the pay of Napoleon. I'm as good an Englishman as any that says that about me: aye, and I've fought the Frogs a deal harder than most of them.' He calmed down, then laughed ruefully. 'Aye, before they threw me out of the army.'

'Whatever for?'

'I'd made sergeant by that time, and we had this great wassack of a lieutenant, fresh out of school, but full of himself. We were out patrolling, and we came across a small group of French cavalry. Not many, mind, but enough to cut us to ribbons if we weren't careful. "Charge," says this wassack. "Give over," say I, because I could see we had no chance against them that way. "Charge or I'll have you shot for mutiny" says the lieutenant, so I knock him out, and I lead the men round the back through the trees, and we capture the whole French patrol. Well, weren't there a right to-do when we got back! Half of them were for having me shot, and the other half were for having me made an officer. They settled on throwing me out.'

'So then you came back home.'

'Aye. I'd a bit saved up, and I took my time about getting back. Looked about me. That's when I saw what were happening in England: what the poor were suffering when the rich were—' He stopped himself. 'Sorry, friend Shirley, that's enemy talk. Ask me summat else.'

'You say you had something saved up?'

He threw his hands up in mock disgust. 'Tell a woman you've a bit of brass, and she's after you like a ferret on a rat!' He preened himself. 'Aye, I'm a man of fortune. I have – wait for it – ninety-five pounds, seventeen shillings and tuppence ha'penny. There! Doesn't that impress thee?'

'There was I, believing you were poor. You're a fraud as well as a rogue.'

'It makes a difference. It means I don't starve if I don't work, and that means I've more time to plan things, to do things. That's one of the reasons they chose me as the leader. It'll last me two year, I'll tell you.'

It wouldn't last me two months. 'And after that?'

'What? Tha thinks I've two year more before I get hung?'

'You're not giving up the fight after last night?'

'Nay.'

'I wish you would.'

'Tha's a mill-owner. Of course tha wishes I would.'

'That's enemy talk, friend Tom.'

'Sorry, friend Shirley,' he said, then added, 'I've talked about me; what about thee?'

I told him a few stories about my background, conscious that every word was pointing up the differences between us. I happened to mention Sir Philip Nunnely, and he broke in.

'Tha means that long streak of – that *gentleman* tha's betrothed to?'

'Yes. I am engaged to be married to Sir Philip,' I said stiffly.

'Lass, isn't there any other man in the whole of England tha could have picked?'

'Sir Philip is kind and gentle and he loves me.' I was beginning to get sick of those words, I'd said them so often.

'And rich.'

'That's not fair.'

'I'm sorry, love. It's nowt to do with me who tha chooses to wed.'

'No, it isn't.'

There was a very long silence.

I broke it. 'Now then,' I said in a voice full of breezy cheerfulness. 'You must rest: and I must too. While I'm asleep, you're not to go wandering around the house, and you're to stay away from the windows. Someone may come visiting. Tartar will wake me if they do.'

He obediently lay back, and I could see the fatigue on his face. 'This is thy bed. Where wilt tha be?'

'In the room next door.'

I remembered that I couldn't lock the door between us from my side, and perhaps the thought showed on my face, for his voice was reassuring as he said, 'Sleep well – friend Shirley.'

'Sleep well – friend Tom.'

I woke late in the afternoon. You may think, reader, that the first thing I did was to open his door gently and look tenderly on his sleeping form: but if you think that, then you are not a woman who has spent two days and a night in the same dress without having had time to wash or brush her hair.

All my other clothes were in the room with him, except the ones in the laundry: those were cleaner than the ones I had on, but equally crumpled. I had to do my own ironing, dress my own hair, and prepare my own food. I learned to respect the skills of my servants, so far ahead of mine, and I resolved to do something about the drab little room in which they lived.

So it was dusk when at last I felt fit to open his door gently and look tenderly on his sleeping form.

He didn't even have the grace to be sleeping. Instead he was ruefully looking at his shirt and jacket: torn and bloodstained.

'It'll have to be this,' he said, picking up the horse-blanket that had so usefully made him look like a pile of old sacking.

'Take them with you, all the same. I don't think I can find a good explanation to the washer-woman of bloody and bullet-torn men's clothes.'

'How wilt tha explain these?' he said, pointing to the stained bedclothes.

'Women bleed, friend Tom. Once a month.'

Every inch of him that I could see – and that was a good many inches – went so deep a shade of scarlet that I was reassured that there was still plenty of blood left inside him.

'Well – er – humph . . .' he said after a while. 'I'd best be off, then.'

'Back to the war.'

'Aye. But we'll not attack heavily defended mills again, I'll tell thee.'

'Robert Moore was prepared to defend it even more heavily than you knew. If you'd succeeded in getting in, you would have been met with spiked rollers coming down the stairs at you, and vitriol poured on your heads.'

'What? The bugger! The bloody ruthless bugger!' Then his anger died down, and he smiled at me. 'Aye, and I'll not apologize for my language: tha's shown that tha can shock me more than the other way round.'

We waited until it was completely dark, then I lit a candle and guided him down the back stairs. At the foot, just inside the back door, we paused. I was standing on the first step and I could meet him more nearly eye to eye. He took my hand in his. 'I thank thee, friend Shirley.'

'I thank thee, friend Tom, for being my friend today. Lies can be useful.'

'We'll not meet again as friends, tha knows that.'

I could not meet his gaze. 'I know that I don't want to meet as enemies,' I said after a moment. 'But I just don't know whether I want to meet as – as *summat else*.'

'Aye, lass. I understand.' He dropped my hand. I blew out the candle and we waited a few moments in the dark so that his eyes became used to it. Somehow the darkness made me feel his presence even more than when I could see him: I could hear him and smell him so very close to me.

'I don't like to leave thee here alone at night.'

'I have two pistols, a blunderbuss and Tartar. After all, General Ludd, I'm in far more danger while you're here than when you're gone.'

'True enough. And tha's safe from my lads. We don't make war on women.' He opened the back door. We couldn't see any watchers: if there were any, we just had to hope that it was so dark that they couldn't see us.

'Goodbye, friend Shirley.'

'Goodbye, friend Tom.'


Mrs Pryor was very quiet and solemn in the days after she and all the servants returned to Fieldhead. I tried to persuade her to tell me what the matter was, but she only looked grave. I could not ask Caroline for her advice, since she did not visit me. Eventually, one night after supper, Mrs Pryor visibly summed up her resolution, and began: 'Shirley, I know that this may cost me my position, but I must do my duty.'

'Surely you must know me well enough not to think that I would do harm to anyone who was doing their duty: much less to you, my dear Mrs Pryor.'

'You will not like what I have to say.'

'Say it, nevertheless.'

'Well, then. Last Saturday evening, just after dark, Caroline and I were walking up here: we took a short cut, and were approaching the house from the back.' I said nothing. 'The house was in complete darkness, and there was no moon, but our eyes were used to the dark,'

'You saw something that troubled you.'

'It troubled me very deeply when I saw you let a man out of the back door.'

I sank my head in my hands. This was not a consequence I had foreseen: and yet I should have done. There was no reason why Mrs Pryor and Caroline should not have come to Fieldhead that evening to discuss the previous night's events: indeed, there was every reason why they should. Now what was I to do? Neither of them would harm me deliberately: they loved me too well. But I loved them too well to confide in them and involve them in my dangerous course of action.

'You say nothing,' she continued. 'I must be glad that you do not try to lie to me. There was a man, wasn't there?'

I nodded.

'Caroline thought she recognized the features of Robert Moore.' Caroline would see the features of Robert Moore in a bowl of porridge. 'Tartar was with you. He was not barking. I know only two men that he does not bark at: Johnnie and Robert Moore. I don't think the man was Johnnie.'

I found my voice. 'Believe me, on my word, we were friends: only friends.'

'Alone in the house with a man, and you say you were only friends?'

'I swear it.'

'No, don't swear. I believe you. But can you assure me that you did nothing of which I would disapprove?'

*I lay in bed with a half-naked General Ludd.* 'No, Mrs Pryor. You would not have approved of all my actions that day.'

'Caroline was – very upset. I had almost to carry her home

and put her to bed. I stayed with her that night: I could not leave her suffering alone.'

So the consequence of my action was to make my two dearest friends think that I was having immoral relations with Robert Moore. Oh, God. What a mess. What a tangled web we weave when first we practise to deceive.

'Mrs Pryor: of all that you have said, the thought that I have hurt Caroline grieves me most deeply. I can understand why she would not see me, but can you not go to her, tell her that my feelings towards Robert Moore are those of friendship and admiration only? That I have no intention of marrying him?'

'I shall tell her, if you wish it. It may perhaps relieve her feelings a little: though perhaps it may not. Oh, my dear, can't you see that, if that is the case, your actions are even more dishonourable than I thought?'


I was at Sir Philip's one afternoon. At this date I cannot remember who else was there: all I recall is that we ladies and gentlemen were sitting around, talking genteelly while we sipped our tea and nibbled our cakes. Then Mr Helstone rode up, his face busy with dreadful news.

'The Prime Minister has been assassinated!' he cried.

The room was filled with words like "Abominable!' 'Unspeakable!' 'Atrocious!' 'Vile!' Then we heard a strange noise coming from the village. We went out and looked down the hill. We could see men and women dancing round a bonfire, waving their hats in the air.

They were celebrating.

Some of the visitors wanted to leave immediately. None of the servants answered their call, so I went to look for them in the kitchen.

I opened the door, and they stopped moving, as if in a picture. Someone had pinned together tea cloths, making a crude flag in the blue, white and red stripes of the French Revolution. They all had glasses in their hands: I had inter-rupted a toast to the assassin.

We are an army of occupation in enemy territory, I thought. And they hate us.

Even so, I still felt secure personally. 'The Luddites don't make war on women,' he had told me.

I believed him, and walked alone round the woods of Briarfield serenely confident of my own safety. This was why I was surprised and angry rather than frightened when a blanket was thrown over my head, a knife was held at my body, I was forcibly picked up and thrown over a wide shoulder, and a Yorkshire voice I did not recognize said, 'Keep your mouth shut, else it'll be the worse for you.'

I knew better than to struggle against a cropper, which my captor appeared to be, judging from the width of his shoulder and the precision with which he held me firmly but without bruising. There were two of them: I could tell nothing of the other, except that he seemed to be as big as the man who was carrying me.

I was taken into what from the smell appeared to be a cowshed, lifted bodily up a ladder, and thrown in the hayloft. One man pinioned me face down in the hay, hissing, 'Keep your eyes shut when I take this blanket off, bitch. If you see our faces, you die.'

I kept my eyes ostentatiously closed while they removed the blanket and replaced it with a blindfold, and ropes round my wrists and ankles.

'I don't think you want me to die of thirst,' I said when they'd finished tying me up. 'May I have a drink of water?'

One of them lifted me into a sitting position: the other held a cup to my lips. There was a tiny gap at the bottom of my blindfold, through which I could see his wrist with the croppers' mark. 'How long do you intend to keep me here?'

'That depends on him.' He didn't explain who *he* was, but I had an excellent idea.

'He knows you've caught me, does he?'

'Not yet: but he will. He'll be right pleased with us for what we have for him.'

I doubted that very much. My capture appeared to be due to those old reliable qualities: confusion, stupidity, and poor communication.

I heard the men climb down the ladder: one of them went out, presumably to fetch *him*. At this point, I thought, a true heroine would find a convenient piece of glass in the hay, cut herself free, and make her escape. I wriggled around until my bonds were tolerably comfortable and went to sleep.

I was woken by a familiar voice saying, 'Oh, aye. And what art tha going to do with this mill-owner tha's caught?'

'Why, can't tha see it? Our lads are in prison: the mill-owner's up in the hayloft. We offer the buggers an exchange.'

'I don't like it. I don't think tha's thought this through. What if they don't release our lads? What's the plan for yon mill-owner then?' There was a pause, before the familiar voice continued. 'Tha can't let him go to inform. Wilt tha kill him, lad? Can tha do it? Or thee?'

'Don't fash thyself. We took care she didn't see our faces.'

At that there was a mighty roar. '*She*? Why, you—' I learned then how much he had restrained the strength of his language in my company. I learned a few interesting new expressions, too. I thought it best to remind him that there was a lady present, so I drummed on the hayloft floor with my heels.

'Right, lads,' I heard him say. 'Bring her down.'

I heard men's steps climbing the ladder. Strong, delicate hands picked me up and lowered me down the ladder to be caught by another pair of hands: equally strong and delicate, but infinitely more welcome.

To most people of my class, all working men smell the same. But to me, the smell of the men who'd captured me was harsh, hateful, threatening; his was warm, manly, protective.

I could not stand: my feet were numb from my bonds, and I staggered and fell against him.

'Hold her up, lads,' he said. 'I'll untie her feet.' I felt him skilfully untie the rope around my ankles: and I felt a gentle, reassuring hand swiftly caress the scar that I'd always have there, as he would always have the same scar on his arm.

My feet were free, and I could stand by myself. His hands held my arms: I could tell he was facing me as he said, 'Lady, you are my enemy. Do you understand that?'

'I understand.' Yes, I did: I would have to play the game his way on his territory, as he had played the game my way on mine.

'I know you,' he said. 'Last time I saw you was from the wrong end of a loaded pistol.'

'I regret not shooting you when I had the chance, General Ludd.'

He turned me round so that my back was towards him and we faced the other two: his hands still held my arms in a gentle but immovable grip. 'Right, lads, what do you see here?' There was no answer, so he said, 'Come on: what sort of a person am I holding in my hands?'

'A mill-owner,' said one voice.

'Wrong. And thee,' to the other man. 'What dost tha see? Say summat.'

'A woman?' came an almost inaudible mumble.

'Wrong again. What you pair of gormless ha'porths have landed us with is a *heroine*. She's brave, young and pretty. Can't you see what'd happen if we kept her? Every soldier in England would be down on us; every man's hand would be against us; every woman would inform on us; and every last one of us would hang!'

'We didn't think—'

'I know you didn't bloody think! Now I must think for you, to see what to do to get us out of this.' He spoke to me. 'Lady, if you give me your word—'

There was a protest. 'Give her word! Tha'd trust our lives on the word of a mill-owner?'

'If I remember, I won five shilling off each of you on that exact same point last February. Now shut up, and let me finish. Lady, I'll let you go free if you give your word not to report what's happened.'

'Very well, General Ludd,' I said. 'You have my word on one condition—'

'Most folk'd think that they were in no case to make conditions, lady.'

'I'm not most folk. I'll not report this, if your two men will get untwisted – if they'll leave off Ludding and swear the oath of allegiance to the King.'

'You bitch!' he roared furiously, and I don't think he was entirely acting. 'Right, lads. She's given you your choice. Look at her closely now. You can either kill her, or get untwisted. Which is it to be?'

There was no sound for a long drawn out moment. I could feel the palms of his hands sweating on my arms: he was frightened. He'd neatly side-stepped being forced to choose between me and his cause. Had I gone too far and forced the choice back on him? And what would he choose if he had to? For the first time, I became frightened too.

'Could you do it?' he continued. 'Could either of you take your knife and cut this pretty throat?' I felt his finger sweep across my neck as he said it. 'Well, could you?'

There was a mumble. 'Nay. I couldn't.'

An even quieter mumble. 'Nay.'

'Right, then. Before tomorrow night falls, the pair of you will go along to the magistrates and untwist yourselves.' He untied my wrists and pulled the blindfold off my eyes. 'Now, lady. What do you see?'

I blinked in the light. 'Nothing more than two loyal subjects of the King.'

I heard a protest. 'She's seen our faces!'

He strode over to them. 'She'll keep her word. And you two –' he said, grabbing each of them by the collar and hauling them off their feet '– will keep yours. Right?'

'Right.'

A nod from the other one.

He kicked open the cowshed door, threw them out, and slammed the door behind them. We heard their footsteps running away, and said nothing until they were safely out of earshot.

Then he said, 'Bloody hell!' and massaged his wounded shoulder, his face a grimace of pain. 'I shouldn't have done that last trick.'

'It was very impressive, lifting two of them like that.'

'It's easy if you've the knack of it. But not with a busted shoulder.' He shook his head at me, smiling ruefully. 'Lass, lass, did tha have to cost me two of my lads?'

'You told me that I was your enemy.'

'Aye, but not that much of an enemy, love!'

'Anyway, I don't imagine they're any great loss, those two.'

'I can't afford to lose any man at the moment, even those two dummocks. Your folk are winning. Half my lads are getting untwisted, and the other half are getting desperate and doing daft things like that pair.'

'Can't you control your men?'

'Control a cropper? Nay, lass, I've never tried. But I can't always get them to see what's right any more. Your folk are threatening blood and murder at them, and they're threatening blood and murder back. And some buggers are taking our name and using it to cover common theft. It's not what I wanted.' He sighed. 'But I shouldn't be telling thee this, tha mill-owner. Come on, I'll walk home with thee, in case any other lad gets a bright idea.'

I stumbled as I stepped forward: my feet were still a little numb and uncomfortable. 'Did they hurt thee? I'll have their guts for garters if they did.'

'Keep your stockings up some other way. I'll be fine in a moment.'

'Shall I carry thee?'

'No, I can walk. But I'd welcome your arm to lean on.'

We set off back to Fieldhead, arm in arm like a respectable married couple taking a stroll after church. It was a beautiful day in early summer: the birds sang and the butterflies fluttered by. I did not need his arm after five minutes walking, but I did not let it go: the strength of him delighted me. We'd met as enemies that day. Would we part as *summat else*? I still didn't know my own mind.

Suddenly he stopped and let my arm fall. He knelt down and picked something up from the ground. He looked up at me, his face distressed.

'Ah, see this.' In his huge hands was a half-formed chick, its beak gaping open and cheeping. 'It's a daft gollin that's fallen out of its nest. Can tha see where it came from? If I can't put it back, I'll have to wring its neck, poor little mite. I'll not leave it to starve or be eaten by a fox.'

'You can't walk by even a little bird, can you?'

'I wish I hadn't seen it. But since I did. . . .'

I studied the cheeping, gaping chick with fellow feeling. Last

137

November, he'd seen me menaced by a mad dog. He'd wished he hadn't seen me, no doubt, in the months of dread that had followed: but since he had. . . .

I looked up at the branches above our heads. 'There!' I said, pointing. 'Is that the nest? Just there, second branch up, towards the end?'

'Hast tha got a hanky? Summat soft to wrap it in when I climb?'

'No. I don't usually bring my reticule when I'm kidnapped. But here—' I turned away from him, lifted my skirt and tore a bit of trimming off my petticoat: in any case, it'd never be the same again after my sojourn in the hayloft.

With his delicate cropper's touch he wrapped the bird in the cloth and tucked it into his shirt, and with his great cropper's strength he hauled himself up the tree. He reached the branch and started moving along carefully, but even with his care it swayed and bent dangerously.

'It won't bear your weight,' I said, starting towards the tree trunk. 'Help me up, and I'll climb along the branch.'

He reached down and pulled me up. I sat astride the branch, my skirt riding up my legs. I blessed the fashion of the age: light, loose cotton. My mother could never have done this in her stiff brocade. He handed the little chick to me, and gripped me as I scrambled along the branch towards the nest. He didn't need to tell me that he wouldn't let me fall: I knew it with my whole being.

I reached forward, forward, forward: ah, there! I placed the chick gently in its nest, and wriggled back along the branch.

'If we stay here, very quiet and still,' he whispered, 'happen we'll see its mum come back.'

We sat astride the branch, hardly moving. He was against the massive tree trunk, and I was close to him. Very gently, as if he were only stopping me from falling, his arms came around me.

Very gently, as if I were only resting, I leaned back against him. Perhaps five minutes passed. Neither of us spoke; neither of us moved. I felt his deep, slow breaths stirring the hair at the back of my neck and behind my ear. And I knew.

A bird with a mouthful of food landed on the nest. She gave us a beady, suspicious look, then thrust the morsel into the beak that gaped frantically. A flutter of wings, and she was off looking for the next meal.

I turned my head to look up at him: he beamed delightedly back at me. It was a silly, trivial rescue: sparrows fall every day. But we'd saved this one, and we were content.

'Look around thee,' he said quietly. 'It's right grand.' It was: from our perch we could see the woods and fields stretch all about us. There were a few weavers' cottages a mile away on the left, and up ahead I could see the roof of Fieldhead over the next rise. But otherwise there was no sign of human life.

'It's beautiful,' I sighed.

'Aye. And then we come along, with our *money*, and our *class* and our *fighting*, and we muck it up.' His voice held a bitterness that chimed badly with the beauty around us.

'And if there were no money and class and fighting, what would you do? If everything were always like this?'

An almost silent groan ripped through him and he looked away into the distance. 'Oh, lass, tha knows, surely?'

'Say it now,' I urged him. 'There's no money and class and fighting here. Just us.'

'Well, then. If it were just thee and me—' His eyes met mine: they were sad, but his mouth was smiling. 'I'd tell thee that I loved thee, and I'd ask thee to marry me.'

'And I'd tell you that I loved you too, and I'd say yes.'

I put my face up, expecting him to kiss me. But he did not. I could see that he was fighting a great battle within himself; then he shook his head sorrowfully and said, 'Nay, I'll not kiss thee, though my whole body aches to. Tha says there's no money and class and fighting here, but look yonder.' He pointed to the row of weavers' cottages. 'That's the sort of place I come from. Now look there,' pointing to the roof of Fieldhead in the distance. 'That's thy place. Even if I weren't a law-breaker, even if I were in work, how could I ask thee to come and live with me there, in one of those cottages, on my thirty shilling a week?'

'You could come and live with me there, in Fieldhead, on my thousand pounds a year.'

'There's a name for men that live on women's money, and it's not one I want given to me.'

I hadn't thought of that. It seemed like stupid pride to me, but not to him.

'Does that matter so much to you? It wouldn't matter to me. Besides, if you married me, it'd be your money.'

'Oh, aye, love? And what happens when I go along to thy tenant and say, "right, Mr Moore, I own this mill now. Get those frames out and put the croppers back"?'

'But all that: it can't go on for ever.'

'Oh, lass,' he sighed. 'My brave, true, beautiful lady. Even if thee and me weren't enemies, even if I don't finish up on the end of a rope, it wouldn't work. Doesn't tha know I've thought on it ever since I saw thee in thy pretty dress, with a pistol in thy hand and murder in thine eyes, and saw the murder change to laughter when tha knew me? Every night I dream of thee beside me in my bed, till death us do part. And then I wake up, and I think, "Aye, that were a pretty dress. A ball dress. And she'd want me to partner her, in fine stiff clothes that'd strangle me. And she's a kind lass, and she'd not chide me when I stepped on that dress, but she'd look sad. And she'd never even mention the way I write like a clumsy gowk; she'd nobbut write all my letters for me so I wouldn't shame her".'

'I shouldn't think that. I'd think of your strength, and the way you risked a horrible death for me, and the way you can't let a little chick fall from its nest.'

'Aye, and happen that'd keep thee going for a while to hide the shame. And I'd try to change to please thee, because I love thee. And happen I'd do it. Happen I could become a gentleman fit to be thy husband, and know which knife and fork to use, and how to address a bishop: I learn fast. But then I'd not be me. I know tha loves me, and it fills my heart with joy to hear thee say the sweet things tha just did. But tha loves *me*, not the silked-up charming gentleman that I'd become if we were wed.'

I didn't answer him, because I couldn't. I had the terrible feeling that he was right. I'd seen the man, and I'd loved him. I hadn't seen the husband in the years to come.

'Does it have to be that way everywhere, always?' I asked sadly after a while.

'It's the way it is, here in England, now in the year 1812. And so I'll nobbut sit here holding thee in my arms, because I can't bear to let thee go, and we'll watch the mother bird feed her gollin. Look, here she comes again.'

# PART 5

I'm sure that neither Caroline nor Mrs Pryor had anything to do with it, but for some reason there was a rumour in the neighbourhood that I was being courted by Robert Moore. Little old ladies would sigh that he was such a fine man, so handsome, and wish us happy. Middle-aged clothiers would smile and say that he was a lucky dog, and wish they were twenty years younger so that they could give him a run for his money.

I was wondering whether I should stitch a sampler saying, 'I am betrothed to Sir Philip Nunnely, who is kind and gentle and loves me,' and hang it up in my parlour, to save me the effort of saying it so often.

Yes, reader, I was still betrothed to Sir Philip. I could not marry the man I wanted to, so why not stay with a man who at least wanted to marry me?

Then one evening Robert Moore came to visit. He was shining. His boots were polished so that you could see your face in them, his teeth gleamed in the candlelight, his hair was glossy and smooth, his neck-cloth was starched so white it made your eyes blink. But overall, he shone from his body and his face, as if a medieval painter had wanted to show that he had received a vision from God.

He made an excuse to be alone with me, and began: 'Miss Keeldar, I am saved! The clothiers put up a collection for me, after

I defended the mill and showed that the Luddites could be defeated. I have three thousand pounds!'

I was sincere in my congratulations. I admire courage and resolution, and he had them in abundance – and it was my property, after all. He showed me the figures that indicated that now the mill would be profitable even if the Orders in Council were not rescinded (though it looked very much as if they would be). He offered to repay the money he owed me, but I refused: it made no sense, since the interest he was paying was better than I could get while being lower than he would find elsewhere, and he could use the money to expand further.

I was very happy for him, and I showed it.

'Miss Keeldar – Shirley, may I call you. . . ?'

'Yes, of course – Robert.'

'Shirley, now I am clear, now I can no longer be accused of seeking a wealthy wife, may I ask you for your hand in marriage?'

My first thought was *poor Caroline*. My second was to rue the way that my wealth appeared to discourage the best men from wanting to marry me. My third was to wonder how to turn him down tactfully: I still wanted to continue seeing him, and he was a good tenant and a fine clothier.

'I am betrothed to Sir Philip Nunnely, who is kind and gentle and loves me.'

'Sir Philip is a weakling who is not worthy of you. You know that: why do you stay with a man who lies down and lets you walk all over him?'

I had a suspicion that he would have no objection to a woman who lay down and let him walk all over her.

'Robert, please don't continue in this fashion. Your suit has no chance.'

'Why not? Shirley, why not?' He put his hands out and came towards me.

'Because I am in love with another man. Is that not sufficient reason?'

'You can't be!' He gripped my arms – hard, so I had a bruise for days afterwards – and studied my face intently. 'You are, aren't you?'

'Yes.'

'How can you love that poltroon? You need a man, a real man.'

I said nothing. Robert Moore would think I was in love with Sir Philip, and everyone else would think I was in love with Robert Moore. Life was getting complicated.

He shook his head, amazed. 'How can I show you what he is: what I am?'

'Robert, please believe me when I say that I admire and respect you. But I wish to remain only your landlord and your friend.'

'Very well, I accept defeat – for the moment. But you know that I am a hard, determined, resolute man, and I always get what I want in the end.'

As he left, I wondered why I didn't feel sorrier for him. Then I realized: he had never said that he loved me.

I told Mrs Pryor in confidence about Robert's proposal and my rejection of it. Her first thought was for Caroline, her second for me.

'Oh, my dear,' she said. 'If you don't love him, if you don't want to marry him, how could you do what you did when we saw him that night?'

I couldn't bear her disappointment in me: she, who had been my governess, the nearest I'd had since my childhood to a mother. No! it was not to be endured.

'Mrs Pryor, will you swear not to reveal what I have to say to any other person? That includes Caroline: it would do her little good in any case since Robert seems determined to pursue me.'

'I swear, if you insist.'

'It wasn't Robert.'

'But Tartar wasn't barking. It can't have been – oh, surely not – not Johnnie?' Her face was filled with revulsion at the thought that I might have that sort of intimacy with a man from the working classes.

'No, no, it wasn't Johnnie,' I replied, to her immense relief. 'Don't press me any further about who he is: all I shall tell you is that he is a fine, strong, good man. He loves me, and I love him.'

'Do you intend to marry him?'

'No. There are reasons—'

'He's married already, isn't he?'

I said nothing: it was a convenient mistake.

'Have you – Shirley, have you done anything wrong?'

'I have done many things wrong. Do you mean: have I lain with him?'

'I shan't pretend to be shocked. That's exactly what I mean.'

'He hasn't even kissed me,' I said sadly.

Mrs Pryor jumped up. 'Oh, my poor, dear girl,' she said tenderly as she put her arms round me to comfort me. 'You know that there is no future for you together, don't you?'

*I'm in love with a man who thinks he'll be hanged in the next two years.* 'Oh, yes,' I said. 'I know there's no future for us together.'

Some days later it was my turn to comfort her. She had returned from a visit to Caroline, and her lips were quivering with the effort of not crying.

'My dear Mrs Pryor, what's the matter?'

'She's dying!' she sobbed.

'Who? Caroline?' She nodded. 'My God, what's the matter with her? Has she seen a doctor? What does he say? Quick, I must go to her at once.'

'No, no, don't go. Your visit would only upset her more.'

'You mean – Robert Moore? She's dying for love of Robert Moore?'

'The doctor hums and haws and talks of a wasting fever, but yes, at bottom, that's what it is.'

'Nobody dies for love!'

'They die for lack of it. Think of her, with her cold, hard uncle, in love with another cold, hard man. Neither of them pays her anything but the briefest attention. She does not want to live, and so she's dying!' She cried bitterly onto my shoulder.

'There's something more, isn't there? Something you haven't told me.'

'Oh, Shirley, haven't you guessed?'

'Guessed what?'

'She's my daughter.'

Between sobs, embraces and cups of tea, she told me the story. She had fallen in love with James Helstone, the rector's brother. After their marriage, she discovered that he had different qualities from the handsome face and charming manner that had attracted her to him: he drank, he kept mistresses, and he was brutal. Her love for him quickly vanished, and was lavished on the only good thing to have come out of their marriage, their daughter. She could obtain no relief from him: the law would give her grounds for divorce only if he had brought his mistresses into their home, which he never had. The cruelty was not so gross as to attract attention: it was the small, mean, continuous kind: slaps and pinches rather than bloody assaults.

At last she left him, taking the infant Caroline with her. That, in the eyes of the law, made her the guilty party. He could obtain a divorce from her: what was infinitely worse was that the law gave him custody of Caroline. Even when he died, Caroline's mother could not get her child back, and Caroline was handed over to her uncle, the upright, unloving rector of Briarfield.

149

'So there was never a Mr Pryor?'

'No, my dear. I took on a new name.'

'But how did you come into my uncle's house?' It was inconceivable that my respectable uncle would take a divorced woman as governess to his daughters and niece.

'That was your dear, kind mother. She knew my suffering: she raged against the injustice of it. She gave me a reference to Mr Sympson so I could earn my living in a new place. When she died and you came into your uncle's household, I paid my debt to her in the only way I could, by trying to take her place and providing for you the love that she would have given you.'

'And you did, Mrs Pryor, you did!' I cried, embracing her. 'But Mr Helstone! Didn't he recognize you when you came back here?'

'The brothers led very different lives: I'd hardly ever met him. Besides, Mr Helstone is not a man to take much notice of insignificant middle-aged ladies.'

Now the vital question, that had hung unasked and unanswered during her narration. 'Does Caroline know?'

'My dear, I don't think it would help her to know that her mother is a divorced woman, and that her father was a cruel, drunken libertine.'

'I think it would help her very much to know that her mother is a kind, warm-hearted woman who has had her own portion of suffering.'

'Do you think so?' Her eyes held a plea to me to say yes, to tell her to go to her daughter, and to give her the love she so much wanted to give, and which Caroline so desperately needed.

I could do it whole-heartedly and sincerely. 'Of course I do. What love has she had, from two cold, stern men? She needs the love of a warm, gentle woman! Go to her. Tell her the truth. It may save her life.'

She needed no more urging. I called Johnnie to drive her in

the cart, for she was in no state to walk. I gave her a fond embrace as she drove off: she had been like a mother to me. Now it was time for her to be a real mother to her own daughter.

I went back into the house, calmly made sure all the doors and windows were closed so no one could hear, stood in the great gloomy hall, and screamed.

'The injustice of it! The law that gives no redress to a good woman married to a bad man! That makes her the guilty party when she leaves him, and that takes her child away from her!

'Oh, mother, mother that I hardly knew, if you are listening now, here in the home where you lived, thank you! Thank you for raging against it, for being willing to lie to save the victim of it! I never knew how much I was your daughter until now!'

I wanted to smash something. I wanted to smash the wicked, man-made law that had caused my friend such suffering. But I could not: there was nothing tangible, nothing physical I could take a hammer to.

I went out the back, picked up an axe, and began chopping wood. Inexpertly, I know (in hindsight, I realize that I am lucky to have all my fingers and toes), but most satisfactorily.

This was what the Luddites felt. They could not smash poverty, but they could smash frames. They could not break the Combination Acts, but they could break a mill window.

I chopped, as if with each blow of my axe I was chopping away at an injustice.

*That!* was for the wicked unfairness of the divorce laws.

*That!* was for poverty: for men not being able to feed their children.

*That!* was for children working all day, because they were cheaper to employ than their fathers.

*That!* was for rich men in Parliament making laws for the rest of us, for women and for poor men.

And *that!* and *that!* and *that!* were for money and class and fighting, that kept apart a man and a woman who loved each other.

Johnnie returned and stared at me in surprise. 'Shall I do that, ma'am?'

I looked at him for a moment. How right Mrs Pryor was to be revolted at the thought that I would have anything to do with him, though for the wrong reasons. For Johnnie was *servile*.

When he had driven back with me from the outbreak of revolutionary fervour I had seen at Sir Philip's after the Prime Minister had been assassinated, he had grovelled that he was not part of it, he had cringed about how much he disapproved of it, he had prostrated himself and told me that he would never have anything to do with that sort of thing. If he had thought it would have helped he would have rolled over on his back exposing his throat as Tartar did when he was in trouble.

Of course he was servile: he was a servant. I was wrong to blame him: I was part of the army of occupation that had made him that way. I would have respected him if he had said, 'Aye, we were celebrating. Our thoughts are our own, and if we do the work that you pay us for, then you have no right to complain.' It was not his fault that he didn't do it: it was mine. I despised him, and I despised myself for despising him.

How much better than either of us were the men who did not grovel, who picked up their Enochs and smashed something. Yes, even the men who had kidnapped me, for they were trying to do something about it.

Well, I would do something about it too. No smashing, no melodrama: all I would do was make life a little easier for a few people in the area of my responsibility. Other people had their own ways of doing something about it, that might be better or might be worse: but this would be mine.

I went into the parlour and wrote to Robert Moore, asking him to find the costs of reducing the children's hours to no more than ten hours a day with no lowering of their earnings, of giving them good meals, time to eat them in and even time to play, and of providing schooling and apprenticeships so that they would be fit for something when they grew too old for child wages. I finished by telling him to take the costs out of the rent he paid me. In the short run, it would mean that even more children would clamour to work in the mill. In the long run, perhaps it would set an example. Even if it didn't, at least the children in my mill would be better fed and taught, and they would see the sun.

*Sunday*, the note had said, so I drove the cart to Robin Hood's Tower after church. He helped me down from the cart, and held me in his arms for just a moment. Then he let me go.

'Nay, I mustn't. Not today, especially; it's as a mill-owner that I want to talk to thee, not as the lass I love.'

'What is it?'

'I hate to do this, because it's mixing up loving and Ludding, but I'd not forgive myself if there were a chance to save my lads and I didn't take it. Lady, there are four men sentenced to hang for attacking your mill. If you wrote to your friend the Lord Lieutenant—'

'Asking for mercy for them? Of course. I'm ashamed that I didn't think of it myself. I'd do it even if I weren't in love with General Ludd.'

'I thank you, lady. I thank thee, lass.'

'It'd be better if the letter didn't come only from me. I'll ask Robert—'

'Robert, is it?' He turned away in pain. 'I'd heard talk of it, but I didn't believe it.'

'Robert Moore asked me to marry him, and I turned him down. I told him that I was in love with another man, which is true, and I told him that I was betrothed to Sir Philip Nunnely, which is also true. What he makes of those two statements is his business.'

'Robert Moore, Sir Philip Nunnely, the Prince Regent: it's nowt to do with me who tha weds. If I can't have thee, can I begrudge another man?' He shook his head. 'Aye, but I do begrudge him. Lass, if tha must have someone, make it Moore. I can work up a good hate for him. But being jealous of Nunnely – it's humiliating!'

'Jealousy's not a pleasant thing, is it?' I tried to change the tone of our talk. 'Tell me,' I said lightly. 'Do I have anyone to be jealous of? A fine strong man like you must have had some interest shown in him.'

He accepted the change. 'Aye,' he said proudly. 'I get letters from the wives of half the House of Lords. I think they must be in love with me: why else would they beg me to murder their husbands?'

'Seriously, was there anyone?'

'Aye. There were a right pretty lass who said she loved me: until I lost my job. She wed another man and she's got two bairns now. Then there were the Peninsula: soldiers don't just *fight*,' he added lasciviously.

I told him of my proposal for the mill children, and he approved and made some suggestions. About apprenticeships, he said, 'Not cropping. There's no future in it, I can see that. If I had a son and I wanted him taught a trade, I'd look at him becoming a mechanic.'


'My dear,' said Mrs Pryor some days later. She looked blooming: not with youth, but with the bloom of middle age. Caroline had responded as I knew she would: with gratitude and love, and above all with a slow return to health. 'I have been neglecting my duties to you. And you, my dear child, have let me neglect them. But now I must speak with you about your happiness.'

'Mrs Pryor, you look serious.'

'I am serious. I must ask you something: what are you going to do about Sir Philip?'

'I have wondered about that myself. I should be grateful for your opinion.'

'I think that you should break your engagement, my dear.'

That was Sir Philip's last supporter gone. Everyone else whose opinion I valued, from Earl Fitzwilliam to Caroline Helstone (including Tom Mellor and Robert Moore, though these two could be accused of bias), had indicated in one way or another that he was not a suitable husband for me. Only Mrs Pryor, from a now completely understandable regard for kindness and gentleness, had approved the match.

'I like being betrothed to him: it means that I am not pestered by young men in quest of an heiress.'

'You like being betrothed to him. Does that mean that you want to marry him?'

'No.'

'Then you are hardly being fair to him, are you?'

'No.'

'Then you will break your engagement to him, as kindly and as gently as he deserves.'

'Yes, I shall, at the first opportunity. And thank you for your advice: for its good sense and mild delivery.'

She sighed. 'Some day, my dear, you will find the right man for you. Someone who combines the kindness of Sir Philip with the strength of Mr Moore.' It must have been written on my face that I thought I'd already found him, for she added, 'A *single* gentleman.'

Single he was; gentleman he was not.

'I don't know. I look around me: how many examples of a happy marriage do I see?'

'That's because you don't remember your mother and father. They were very happy.'

'Oh, well. I shall not argue.' I didn't wish to pain her by pointing out that she was hardly in a position to advocate marital bliss. 'But at least we are agreed that it is not Sir Philip Nunnely with whom I shall find happiness: he must find someone else – perhaps there is even a pretty, warm-hearted young lady in the world who will like his poetry!'

It seemed so easy to say that I would break off my engagement. But I found that I could not. Every time we met, I would think, 'This is the time. I shall do it . . . in a moment.' Reader, you will not think me guilty of self-flattery if I say that I was a brave woman: I had held a hot iron to my flesh, I had whisked a man from under the noses of the militia, I had endured three months of dread without (much) complaint. But I was not brave enough to meet Sir Philip's loving eyes, and tell him that our engagement was over.

Robert Moore wrote me a letter asking if he might see me about my plans for the mill children. I knew that there would be some embarrassment in our first meeting after I had rejected his proposal, but it would have to be done, and this was as good a time as any.

Neither of us made mention of our previous meeting; we settled straight down to business. He was in whole-hearted approval.

'I am not a cruel man. I don't like seeing children working twelve hours a day. But I haven't had anything to spare until now.'

He had his own ideas, and he showed them to me: better ideas than mine, such as an eating hall where the food could be bought wholesale, so that all the workers, not just the children, could get better meals at a lower price than they could find elsewhere.

'Well-fed workers are harder workers,' he said.

I was surprised how little more everything would cost, if things were planned intelligently – and if he kept the frames, and didn't have to pay croppers thirty shillings a week.

I made the suggestion of apprenticeships for mechanics – without, of course, saying where the idea came from – and he accepted it.

'Yes! We can never get enough good ones, and there'll be an increasing need for them. It'll infuriate the Luddites, of course, but I defy them! Why are you smiling like that?'

'Oh, nothing, nothing,' I said hastily. 'I was just pleased that you approved of the idea.'

I had never liked him better than I did that morning: enthusiastic, with a vision of a world where even the poorest wore good warm Yorkshire wool clothing. It occurred to me that this was, perhaps, part of some strange courtship: that he was giving me his plans as another would have given me flowers. If so, it was working: I became engrossed in them, making my suggestions and asking questions. Drainpipes and interest rates were far more to my taste than poetry and bon-bons.

His ambition, his dream, was to own a mill: not mine, built twenty years ago, but his own, modern mill, with modern machines, and a modern power system. 'Water mills are fine, and they have their purpose: but you should see the new steam engines! The power in them! This one: look, it's the latest design from Boulton and Watt!' As he talked of shafts and cylinders and pistons his face became transfigured with passion. 'There's so much progress: before long someone will invent a broadloom for wool, like there is already for cotton, and I want to be ready for it. We won't have to depend on the weavers any more. We're conquering the old ways, that depended on nature and people. Now we've got power at our command, unlimited power! It's the future of the world!' He seized my hand. 'Come with me,

Shirley, come with me into the future as my wife! With you by my side I could rule the earth!'

'Robert – Mr Moore. I am sorry, but I must ask you to stop talking that way. Now,' I said, pointing to the design, 'what were you saying about centrifugal governors?'

He answered me: but not before saying, 'I shall have you, Shirley. You can't deny me.'

We were still bound together in our discussion when Sir Philip was announced. There was nothing on the surface to show any tension between the two; nothing in their words that would indicate that they were rivals.

'Oh, Shirley,' Robert said as he rolled up the designs. 'I'm taking a few people round the mill tomorrow evening: they are important to my plans. Would you like to come?'

I agreed, then Robert turned to Sir Philip and said, 'And you, sir. Perhaps you would like to accompany Miss Keeldar?' Then he rattled off a list of people who would be coming, names of solid respectability.

I did not like this. There was never any reason for Robert to be polite to Sir Philip, and especially not now. I believed that Robert would like to – to what? To push him in the mill race in front of half the worthies of the West Riding?

I stifled my doubts. 'Oh, Robert, before you go, one more thing,' I said, producing the letter that I had written to Earl Fitzwilliam asking for mercy for the men who had attacked the mill. 'Will you add your signature to mine? It'll carry more weight if you do.'

He scanned the letter, then threw it down. 'I said I was not a cruel man. I didn't say I was a merciful one. Let them hang!'

When he had left, Sir Philip sighed, and looked at me with the eyes of a spaniel puppy. 'I've heard a rumour – they say – Oh, Shirley, tell me it's not true! Tell me that you won't leave me for that man.'

This is the moment, I thought. But I couldn't do it. And when I said that I'd not leave him for that man, and he embraced me with all the passion he felt for me, I raged against my cowardice, my folly, and my deceit.

Sir Philip and I walked down to the mill together arm in arm next day. It was near midsummer, and the evening was warm and long. Robert greeted us at the mill gates. He left them open for the rest of the party, saying, 'The dogs are tied up, but they'll give us warning if anyone comes.'

He let us in through the counting-house door, which he locked behind him.

'You're the first to arrive,' he said. 'While we're waiting for the others, shall I show you round the mill, so I can explain my plans better?' I did not like this at all, but could I say, *Mr Moore, I fear you'll murder Sir Philip, so let's not bother*?

When Robert opened the door from the counting-house to the main section of the mill, and I saw the machines ahead of us in the evening light, I knew that I must not let Sir Philip enter. I had not been round the mill since my visit the previous December, but I remembered the giant mill wheel, the great shafts of metal, the heavy wheels inside. And I thought also of spiked rollers and carboys of vitriol.

'No, let's stay here,' I said, frantically searching for an excuse. 'Some of your visitors might be offended if they had to wait for you to let them in.'

It was feeble, but he accepted it. 'Very well. Let me offer you some hospitality.' He took from the cupboard some cakes and bottles, and offered them to us. And I made sure that everything Sir Philip ate and drank was also sampled by Robert or me.

We conversed for a while about his plans. Robert was intelligent and well-informed; Sir Philip was ignorant and patronizing. I wanted to shout out, *Let's stop all this nonsense! I don't want to marry either of you, but if I must have one of you I'll choose Robert.* But I did not.

It was by now nearly dark. 'Robert,' I asked. 'Where are the rest of your visitors?'

'They aren't coming,' he said calmly. 'I lied.'

'I suspected as much. Sir Philip, let's leave.'

Sir Philip jumped up out of his chair. 'This is outrageous, Moore! What do you mean by it?'

'You have something I want,' Robert said. 'I intend to take it from you.'

'What? What is all this nonsense?' Sir Philip blustered. 'Moore, I demand that you unlock this door at once!'

'Very well.' He took the key out of his pocket, walked over to the door to the outside, and unlocked it. I breathed a sigh of relief, and started to leave.

Then Robert gripped my arm hard. 'Sir Philip,' he said. 'You may leave at any time you want.'

'This is absurd, Robert,' I said. 'Let me go and stop acting like the villain in a melodrama.'

'You're most acute, Shirley,' he replied. 'That's exactly what this is. I have tried reason with you: now we'll act out a little drama and see who turns out to be the hero, and wins the hand of the beautiful heroine.'

Sir Philip paled. 'I am not a fighting man,' he said.

'I know that,' said Robert. 'That's why the stage is set to be completely fair to each of us.' He reached into a drawer and pulled out a pistol; then, still gripping me firmly, he set it down on a table a little way away from the other man. He took a few steps back, pulling me with him. 'There, Sir Philip. It is mid-way between us. You have a choice. You may leave at once, alone. Or you may seize the pistol and threaten me with it, perhaps even shoot me if necessary, and take Miss Keeldar with you. But take note: if you make a move towards the pistol, I shall too. And I may seize it first, and threaten you, and perhaps even shoot you. Now, which is it to be?'

Up until this point I had not acted. I had been trying to break my engagement to Sir Philip for some time: now Robert was doing it for me. Melodramatic, certainly, but effective. And I had, after all, thought that if I had to choose between them, I would choose Robert. So when I said, 'Don't be ridiculous, Robert, you can't force me to marry you,' it was only a token protest.

If at that point he had said something like, *I know that, I'm just getting rid of this poltroon so that you're free*, I might in the end have accepted him. But he did not. Instead he said, 'But I can force *you.*'

'What?'

'Let's make quite clear what's at stake. If Sir Philip reaches the pistol before I do, you can go with him. If he walks out on you, he is leaving you here with me. And I shall have your promise to marry me before you leave. Willingly, I hope. The alternative is that I take you by force, and the shame of it will make you accept me.'

I was so shocked I couldn't speak. My thoughts, my feelings were in turmoil. I couldn't believe that this was happening, that he was serious, but I also knew that it was happening, and that he was serious. And I realized that though a woman may be as brave, as intelligent and as resolute as a man, he is physically stronger than she is. If he is mad enough to want to, a man can always take a woman by force.

'So, Sir Philip,' he jeered. 'The choice is yours. Are you going to be the hero, and save the heroine from the villain? Or are you going to run home to Mummy and leave her in his clutches? She's beautiful, Sir Philip, isn't she? Look at her. What's she worth to you? Are you man enough to risk your life for her?'

At last my thoughts returned to some sort of order: I was in control of myself, if not of the situation. If Sir Philip and I could act together, there was no danger. I could struggle with my captor, and put up enough of a fight to distract his attention while Sir Philip went for the pistol.

If it had been Tom Mellor there, a tiny gesture, a phrase with extra meaning, would have been enough to communicate with each other and work together. But if Tom Mellor had been there he would by now have smashed the pistol and be tearing Robert Moore apart. All I had to save me was Sir Philip Nunnely.

'Please help me, Sir Philip,' I begged. 'Don't leave me alone to struggle with him. You must save me. You must act *now*!' I shouted as my fingernails went for Moore's eyes, I butted my head at his throat and tried to knee him in the private parts.

Then my wrists were gripped, and Moore was laughing. 'Yes, Shirley, that would have worked, if only you'd had a man worthy of you to help you. If only you'd had a man at all. But look at him! Look at him quivering and shivering!' He laughed again. 'See! He's actually gone and pissed himself!'

I could see the humiliating liquid spreading in a puddle on the floor.

'I'm sorry,' Sir Philip whispered. 'I'm sorry, so sorry. Shirley, forgive me. I couldn't do it.'

He stumbled out of the door. We could see him stagger towards the mill gates, his body racked with sobs, the dogs barking furiously but impotently from their chains.

'Now we have got rid of him, we can— Ah! I should have expected that.' For Moore had unwisely loosened his grip on me for the fraction of the second that I needed to grab the pistol.

'You enjoyed breaking that man, didn't you?' I said with loathing, pointing the pistol at his heart.

'I didn't break him. He did. He had a choice.'

'Do I get one?'

'Of course. Please, Shirley, you must believe my intentions are honourable.'

162

'Honourable? To rape a defenceless woman is honourable?'

'I shall refrain from pointing out that you are far from defenceless at the moment. Shirley, I beg of you – yes, I beg,' he said, falling down on his knees. 'Please say you'll take my hand, say you'll be by my side, say you'll be my guide, my friend, my helpmeet – my wife!'

'Oh, Robert, you fool! If only you'd left me free to choose, if you'd shown some compassion to that poor man, if you'd asked me in all sincerity without the threat of rape, I might have taken you. But not now. Not when I've seen you so brutal, so ruthless.'

He stood up. 'You need a man, Shirley. A real man. You need me.' He started to move towards me, and I jerked the pistol threateningly at him. 'You don't have what it takes. Remember, I've seen you. If you can't shoot that Luddite scum, you can't shoot me.'

'I'd rather marry that Luddite scum than you, Mr Moore, believe me,' I said with the utmost sincerity. 'And believe me also when I say that I'd rather shoot you than marry you. If you don't, you'll be making a fatal mistake.'

He took a step towards me, then another. He was smiling, completely unafraid. 'Get back!' I warned. 'This is your last chance!'

He took one more step. My finger tightened on the trigger, and I fired.

Nothing happened.

'So you do have what it takes, after all.' He took the pistol gently from my hand. 'How fortunate that it wasn't loaded.'

I shook with revulsion at his deception. He'd broken Sir Philip, knowing all time that he was in no danger. I loathed the man from the bottom of my soul.

Well, I could deceive too. 'Robert—' I began.

'Shirley, don't spoil my regard for your integrity by promising to marry me just so that you can walk out of the door and never come back.'

He knew what I was going to do!

'You see, I know you, Shirley. And I shall know whether you are sincere or not.' He held my chin in his hand and forced me to look up at him. 'And I know that deep in your heart you want me. You are a woman: a powerful woman, the only woman in the world worth conquering, but still a woman, and I am the man to conquer you. Some time tonight you will recognize it. You'll know that I am a man, with a man's power. I may take your body, or I may take your mind, but I shall take one of them, and you will know it, and be mine for ever.'

For a perilous moment, I was almost sucked into the whirlpool of his insanity. I could feel its tug, pulling me towards him, to be his. Then, thank God, my sense of humour saved me. *He thinks of me as a Boulton and Watt steam engine.*

'Oh, Robert,' I sighed, and I leaned my head on his chest. 'You have shaken me. Please let me sit down for a moment.'

'Why, yes, of course,' he said, taking my arm tenderly and guiding me to a chair.

'May I have drink of water, please?' He fetched me one, and I drank it slowly, thinking furiously.

Could I get away with lying to him and pretending to accept his proposal? I thought not. I'd been to the edge of the whirlpool and felt its tug, and I knew that if I said, 'Yes, Robert, I shall marry you,' there was a dreadful chance that I might end up doing so. No! If I must be violated, let it be physically and forcibly, not mentally and by my consent.

A scream? No one could hear: in any case, I'd have his hand clapped over my mouth before I could utter a second. Escape or hiding, then.

There were two doors from the counting-house, and both were still open. One led outside, to the mill yard: the other into the mill itself. I weighed up the chances. Outside, he could run faster than I. Inside, he knew the lie of the land better than I. But the mill looked invitingly dark: there were plenty of hiding places for someone small and light on her feet: I could keep hidden all night until the mill opened in the morning. I tried to recall where everything was, from my visit last December; what a pity we had not taken his tour this evening.

'What's that noise?' I said.

For a moment he thought I was trying to trick him: but then it came again. There was a noise outside! Was there anyone out there? The outside door started to look more inviting.

He went to the window. 'Only the dogs after a rat or something. They aren't barking. Were you hoping for a rescue?'

He turned back, and I was gone through the door into the mill: it was closer.

It was almost completely black in the mill. I could just see the shapes of the windows. I could hear the millrace: a quiet ripple of water over the great mill-wheel. It was not much, but it would mask the sound of breathing, or of very light footsteps.

His body was silhouetted against the oblong of light from the door to the counting-house. He stood still, listening, for he could no more see in the dark than I could, and was straining to catch any sound of me over the noise of the millrace.

I looked away from the light so my night vision would improve. On this, the ground floor, were great bales of coarse woven cloth waiting to be finished. Along from me were the fulling and teazelling areas, and beyond them, the cropping shop.

With forty-pound shears with sharp edges. I liked the idea of those very much: I'd seen them hanging on the wall last time I'd been in the mill.

In December, before the frames were put in and the croppers with their shears turned off.

What other available weaponry was there in the mill? Weaponry that I could take, and use with a woman's strength against a strong man? The spinning-mules seemed my best chance, up two flights of stairs from me. Stone stairs, that would not creak with my weight: I blessed my father for installing them.

Moore was still standing in the counting-house doorway, unmoving, listening. Very carefully I pulled my shoes off: light summer pumps, fortunately. I threw one of them down towards the finishing shop: it landed, and Moore was after the sound like a terrier on a rat. I crept silently towards the stairs, my arms in front of me so that I would not bump into anything in the dark. But at the bottom of the steps I hit something small with my foot: it fell down – not loudly, but enough.

Flight, then, as I raced up the two flights of stairs. As I reached the second floor, I hurled my other shoe down into the opening of the first floor, where the weaving looms were. It worked: I could hear that Moore was not following me up, but was searching around the looms of the floor below.

Minutes passed: I took the time to recover my breath, and to find a hiding place behind the mules in case he came up after me. Then I heard his steps going down the stairs again, and into the counting-house. His voice called out: 'I've locked the door, Shirley!'

Oh, well. It had never been much of a choice, unless I could have reached it with a good fifty yards' start on him.

My eyes were now used to the dark, and I could make out the shapes of the machines. I stood up, and felt my way around them, working by touch and poor memory until I felt something sharp. Gingerly I worked at it, taking my time so as not to make a sound. Yes: it was loose. I had no idea what it was called or what it was used for, but I knew what I'd use it for if I had to. I tucked it down the front of my dress.

Now what? I felt the call of the shears. Perhaps nobody had got round to removing them yet: it was worth trying. I tiptoed along the floor to the flight of steps at the other end of the mill. These would bring me straight down into the cropping shop. Silently, carefully, I walked down them.

I reached the bottom: and a lamp was lit.

'I thought you'd arrive here eventually, Shirley,' he said, the lamp lighting his face from below and making him look diabolical. 'The air of rebellion in this one small corner of my kingdom: I knew it would attract you. But I'll remind you that I conquered it.'

It was heavy sharp blades that attracted me, not the air of rebellion: but they were gone with the croppers.

Then I recalled the one last advantage I had over him: my sanity. He was like the mad dog, that I had held with the force of my will and my gaze. I would hold him with the force of my will and my speech. The dog's madness was ended only by a death blow: but perhaps the man could be cured if I got him to talk of drainpipes and interest rates, and reminded him of his one true love, the mill.

'The doors are locked, the windows are barred,' he said, and he started towards me.

'Yes, and I've been meaning to raise the issue, Robert,' I said calmly. 'What would happen in a fire? You've two hundred workers here, and only two doorways. It'd be most dangerous, especially for the people on the upper storeys.'

'Yes, but the stairs are stone: they'd not catch fire.'

I'd got him!

'How long would people be safe there?' And he answered me, and pointed to the buckets of water, and decried the use of timber beams in buildings. And when we'd sorted that out, he explained to me how the frames worked, and how the mechanical shears were joined together (and bolted down, I noticed: pity).

I noticed the maker's name. 'Not made by Enoch Taylor, I see,' I laughed.

'Not Enoch Taylor,' he laughed back. Not a cruel, triumphant laugh, that he'd used to humiliate Sir Philip. Just an ordinary laugh, at a not very good shared joke.

I thought I had almost returned him to sanity, when he said, in a matter-of-fact tone, 'Have you considered my offer, Shirley?'

'The answer is still no,' I said, equally matter-of-factly.

'I'm afraid I can't accept it.'

'I'm afraid you'll have to accept it. I assure you most sincerely that I shall not marry you even if you succeed in raping me.' I reached for the sharp point I'd stowed inside my dress.

'Not rape; just anticipating the pleasures of marriage,' he said.

And then a huge masked form loomed out of the shadows, and one great hand gripped him by the throat while the other gripped his private parts, and a deep, deadly voice said, 'It's not easy for a man to do either when his ballocks are ripped off and shoved down his gullet.'

A blue eye winked at me over the mask. 'Shall I kill him for you, lady?'

The wink, the *you*, the *lady*: they were enough to tell me that he did not want me to hurl myself at him crying, 'Tom! Oh, Tom!' and weep on to his manly chest, which is what I very much wanted to do, and what a proper heroine would have done when saved by the hero from a fate worse than death.

'General Ludd, your arrival is most opportune,' I said instead. 'I am glad, on reflection, that I did not shoot you last February. Do you think you could put my tenant down? He appears to be having some difficulty breathing.'

He wasn't using the trick grip to haul big men off their feet and impress the watchers: he was using a death grip with both hands, and the only reason Moore wasn't screaming in agony was that he was strangling.

'Certainly, lady.' He carried his victim over to the frames and threw him down on them. 'I were going to break these, Robert

Moore. But happen I've done damage enough here for one night.' Then he let go, and Moore was gasping and heaving for breath as he curled up in pain. 'Lady, do you want me to walk you home?'

'I should appreciate it very much, General Ludd. It seems that you are the only true gentleman here this night.' We started to walk out, then I remembered. 'The doors are locked and he has the keys.'

'Keys? Who needs keys?' he said, as he picked up his Enoch and smashed the door open. He took his clogs from his belt where he'd carried them so he could walk silently, put them on his feet, and strapped his hammer on his back. We walked side by side but well apart until we were outside the mill gates.

And then I hurled myself at him crying, 'Tom! Oh, Tom!' But I wasn't weeping on to his manly chest: I was howling with laughter.

Our laughter eventually died down. 'I don't need this,' he said, pulling off his mask. 'Now I can kiss thee properly.'

So he did, and I kissed him back, as if we could cram into a few moments all the kisses that we'd held back for too long. Once, in jest, I'd vowed to fling my arms round the man who'd saved me and kiss him passionately: now at last I kept my word. And his great arms were around me, holding my body to his, neither harshly that crushed the breath out of me, nor feebly that would let me go, but perfectly: strong, gentle man that he was.

His lips left mine and he looked at me with a gladness in his eyes that I knew I reflected. 'My brave, true, beautiful lady. I love thee, lass.'

'I love you too, Tom.'

There was a sound from the mill gates. Moore was standing there, crouching in agony; how he'd managed to drag himself out I don't know. He seemed as devastated by what he'd seen as by Tom's grip. 'You— him—' he gasped through his ruined throat. 'Whore!'

Tom moved towards him, and I believe would have killed him, but I put my hand out. 'I want no blood shed tonight to spoil what we've found,' I said to him, then spoke to Moore.

'You said I needed a real man. I have one. Compared with him, you're as little a man as Sir Philip Nunnely. But you are a good tenant and clothier, and I am happy for you to stay that way. I shall forget everything that happened tonight, if you will also. Oh, except one thing that you really must remember: a man can face the gallows just as much for attempted rape and abduction of an heiress as he can for frame-breaking. Goodnight, Mr Moore.' Then I turned to Tom. 'Take me home, lad.'

'Aye, lass,' he said, as he picked me up off my feet.

'I can walk. You don't need to carry me.'

'I like carrying thee.'

'I do believe you're showing off to me.'

'I like showing off to thee.'

It was very slow progress we made towards Fieldhead that night, interrupted as it was by many kisses, and many foolish words that are of no concern to anyone else. But if, reader, you wonder how he arrived in the nick of time as befits a proper hero, you may be interested in this part of our conversation.

'I were up yon hill looking down on the mill—'

'I think you were spying out the land, General Ludd.'

'Happen I were. And I saw that the mill gates were open, but I couldn't see anybody. "Eh up," I think, "there's a chance for me here," so I come and have a closer look. Then I see the counting house door open, and yon wassack that tha's betrothed to—'

'Yon wassack that I *was* betrothed to.'

'I like that *was*,' he said, kissing me again. 'I tell you, he comes out looking like he'd lost a pound and found sixpence, and I creep in to see what's up.'

'That was you when I heard the dogs make a noise!'

'Aye. They didn't bark, but they made a bit of a fuss. And then I see that somebody's left the door open. "That's right thoughtful," say I, "when here's me with my Enoch all handy." So I step in, and go toward the shearing frames: quiet like, I wouldn't want to interrupt anybody.'

'Of course not. Most gentlemanly of you.'

'And then I hear Moore yell out, "Shirley, the door's locked." And I think I might be in a bit of a bother, because I didn't want to have a fight with him, not then, and not in front of thee. So I find a dark corner, and I wait. And then I hear thee and Moore in the cropping shop, and tha's talking to him about fire precautions and such, and I think it's nobbut a matter of business, even if I do think it were a bit strange to do it in a deserted mill in the middle of the night, so I don't interfere. And even when he were talking about "considering his offer", I still thought it were business. It were only when I realized what kind of offer he were making that I stepped in. Happen I smashed summat much more valuable to him than his shearing frames,' he finished with great satisfaction.

'I don't know. He's more in love with his mill than any woman.'

'He's not in love with thee any more.'

'He never was: I represented power to him, like a new steam-engine.'

'I'm concerned for thee, love. Tha's made an enemy there.'

'So have you.'

'Aye, but I always were. I'm glad tha's got the dog.'

'Tartar likes Robert Moore.'

'Aye, so he does.'

'Don't worry. I'll make sure everything's locked, and I have my pistols. I'll be safe.'

'Aye, tha will, and all. I'm sure of that.'

We finally arrived near Fieldhead. 'This is where I set thee down,' he said, still carrying me in his arms. 'Now, it's thy choice, love, what I do next. Do I walk off, and go about my unlawful business, and meet thee again at Robin Hood's Tower; or do I wait to see a candle in thy bedroom window, and go though the back door, and meet thee again in thy bed?'

How I loved him! How much I wanted to say yes to him, and to feel his arms around me all through the night! But the voices of my education and my principles cried out to me, and I listened to them.

'There'll not be a candle in my bedroom window tonight,' I said sadly. 'Oh, I'm sorry, Tom, but—'

'Nay, nay, love, don't apologize. I must apologize to thee for asking. Where I come from, a lad and a lass don't lie together unless they mean to get wed.'

'Where I come from, a lady and a gentleman don't lie together unless they actually are wed.'

'Aye, and it's best that I don't let a mill-owner lead me astray from the path of villainy.' He set me on my feet. 'So kiss me, love, and say goodnight.'

I was dressing next morning when Mrs Gill told me there were some people who'd come to see me about a job. I went down to find two large working men standing in the hall. It took me a moment to recognize them – I'd been blinking in the light from having a blindfold removed the last time I saw their faces.

I instantly ran for my pistol. 'Stay where you are or I fire.'

'Nay, lady, we're on your side now,' said one, completely unperturbed.

One day, I thought, if I'm very lucky, I'll manage to scare a man when I point a pistol at him.

'You've made an enemy of Robert Moore,' the man continued. 'So that makes us your friends. He says we're to come and keep you safe.' The other one gave him a nudge. 'Oh, aye. He says we've to apologize for kidnapping you. We're right sorry about that, aren't we?' he said to his companion, who nodded.

I was confused. 'He says? Who's he?'

The man shifted his feet uncomfortably. 'You know, lady. Him.'

'Him? Oh, you mean *him*?' This is a very silly conversation, I thought, but I do know who *he* is.

'Aye, him. He says we can't go Ludding any more, and we lost our jobs when the frames came in, so we'd best make ourselves useful and look after you.'

'So he thinks that I – a mill-owner – am safer in the hands of two Luddites who kidnapped me than I am with my own tenant?'

'Aye. Happen he's right.'

Happen he is, I thought, and I put away the pistol. 'Very well. Now, about your wages: I'll pay—'

'No wages.'

'You're not in work: you're looking after me: of course I'll pay you wages.'

'No, he's paying— ow!' he yelled, as the other man kicked him sharply with a beclogged foot.

'Oh, I see. He's paying your wages and he told you not to tell me, is that right?'

'Aye,' he said sheepishly.

That stupid, addle-brained dummock was going to pay these men out of his ninety-five pounds, seventeen shillings and tuppence ha'penny rather than have me spend anything out of my thousand pounds a year! I'd kill him!

'You won't tell him we let it slip, please? He wouldn't like it.'

No, he wouldn't. A man had to protect his woman, and if he couldn't do it himself, he'd pay someone else to do it. I loved him so much! And because I loved him, I'd respect his pride.

'No, I shan't tell him.'

'Thank you, lady,' he said, very relieved.

'He'd batter your heads together, would he?'

'Nay, it's not that. It's. . . .' I could see his face working to express himself. 'Well – you only feel good with yourself when he says you've done the right thing. You know what I mean?'

Oh, yes. I knew what he meant.

That was how I came to have two very large guards. Samuel Haigh was the spokesman of the pair: his brother Abraham communicated mainly by nods and significant nudges, and would mumble something only when those resources failed him. I was concerned how Tartar would react to them, but he greeted them with an enthusiasm that made me wonder how many properties in the district were guarded by dogs who would fend off Luddite attackers only by licking them to death.

I did not want it known around Briarfield that I needed guards, so I set them to work in the garden: my roses and apple trees suffered enormously at their hands. To the many enquiries about why I didn't get rid of them, I would reply that they were untwisted Luddites who'd seen the error of their ways, and that we must ensure that they had work so that they would not fall back into sin. I won a lot of respect for my charitable attitude.

I don't know to this day whether I was in any danger from Robert Moore: I only know that I was never attacked while I had the Haigh brothers with me. I liked having them around; if I could not have Tom by my side, I'd have his proxies.

Above all, they weren't servile. They were willing to obey my orders, so long as they agreed with them. If they didn't, Samuel would soon tell me, while Abraham would simply stand there not doing anything. I managed to stop Samuel whistling *The cropper lads for me* in public, but he carried on doing it when nobody else was around.

They soon became useful in fending off young men. Once it

became known – as it did remarkably quickly – that I was no longer betrothed to Sir Philip Nunnely, and that Robert Moore was out of the running, I was besieged by suitors. Curates, clothiers, captains of the militia all came a-courting: but it was only a brave and determined young man who would get through the defences provided by Tartar and the Haigh brothers.

At long last, one day Caroline came to visit me. I'd heard daily bulletins from Mrs Pryor, and I knew she was getting better. But I would not force my presence on her: in her eyes I was a rival.

She was much thinner than when I'd last seen her: her slightly plump girlish bloom had gone, replaced by a finer wisdom. We embraced, talked about the weather, had some tea and cakes, and then she said, 'I was wrong, Shirley. I know that now. I thought you were my worst enemy: now I know that, in sending my mother to me, you were my best friend.'

'Oh, Caroline, I've missed you. Why wouldn't you believe me when I told you that I had no interest in Robert Moore?'

'I thought he had an interest in you. All the rumours.' Then she held my hand and asked me the hardest question of my life. 'Will you give me your word that he never asked you to marry him?'

What could I say? *Yes, Caroline, he did, and he would have raped me into accepting him*? Could I lie to my best friend to give her comfort? Mercifully, an answer fell into my mind like manna from heaven. 'Caroline, I give you my word that Robert never once told me he loved me.' If she noticed the difference between what she'd asked and what I'd answered, she was too eager to believe me to press any further.

You poor girl, I thought. If he ever decides to marry you, you have as much chance of retaining your selfhood against him as a puff of smoke in a Yorkshire gale. Briefly I wondered whether it was the slightest use to try to make a match between her and Sir Philip, who would be in desperate need of a sweet-tempered, loving woman. But her obsession with Robert Moore was too strong. Besides, I wasn't eager to do favours for Sir Philip: he had, after all, left me to be raped.

One reason she had called was to invite me to a celebration of her birthday: she would be nineteen on the following Monday.

'Will Robert be there?' I asked.

'Oh, yes! It's wonderful. You know my uncle would never have him in the house or even let me visit his sister because of their political differences? Well, since they became allies against the Luddites, Robert is now a welcome visitor. Isn't that marvellous?'

'I'm very happy for you.'

'So will you come?'

Well, he was still my tenant. I had to meet him at some time. A birthday party, with lots of people around us, was as good a place as any to do it. 'Yes, I should be happy to. And I promise you that when you see Robert and me in the same room, you will be assured that I'm the last woman on earth that he'd want to marry.'

*Munday*, said the note. I folded it up and tucked it into my dress, where it warmed me. Of course he was right that if we ever did succeed in getting married I'd write his letters for him; I'd just have to persuade him that it was no harm to his pride, any more than it harmed my pride when he'd saved me from Moore. I could write better than he: he was stronger than I: did it matter?

I wouldn't be able to stay with him long, as I'd promised to help Caroline with preparations for her birthday celebration. I was in the cart about to leave for Robin Hood's Tower when Samuel ran out of the house and started to climb in.

Oh dear, I thought. I'm sure this is a complication that didn't cross his mind when he sent me my guards. 'Samuel, please don't come with me.'

'He wouldn't like it if I let you go alone anywhere.'

*He wouldn't like it if you come with me, that's certain.* 'I don't need you. I'll be quite safe.' Then, when he showed no sign of getting down, I confessed in desperation, 'I'm going to see a man!'

'Oh. Like that, is it?'

'Yes, it's like that. I assure you that he's just as capable of looking after me as you and Abraham.'

'Big strong man, is he?'

'Yes, he is.' *He could pick you up in one hand and your brother in the other and throw you both out the door.*

'And what about the journey there and back?'

'Samuel, go and get me my pistols, and the blunderbuss too, and Tartar as well if you like. But don't come with me. Look, if he ever finds out that you've let me go alone' – *which he will very soon* – 'I'll tell him that it was on my orders, and I'll make it good with him. I give you my word: and you know what that's worth.'

'I suppose he wouldn't like it if we stopped you courting,' Samuel admitted reluctantly. *You don't know how right you are!*

Eventually he obeyed me, and I drove the cart to Robin Hood's Tower loaded like an artillery wagon.

He confessed that this problem hadn't occurred to him.

'If we want to keep on seeing each other, we'll have to let Sam and Abe know,' he said, biting his lip.

'Can they keep a secret?'

'Abe can, of course: get more than two words out of him in any one day and it's a miracle, but Sam likes the sound of his own voice. And we can't tell Abe without Sam.'

'What would your lads think if they found out about us?'

'What? Me courting a mill-owner? They wouldn't be happy about it, I'll tell thee.'

'In that case, I'll just have to come alone.'

'Nay, love, I couldn't let thee do that.'

'Tom, look at me!' I cried, exasperated. 'Remember me? I'm the woman who held a pistol to you, who put a hot iron to her flesh, who got you out from the militia! I can look after myself for an hour!' When he didn't reply, I put my arms round his neck and said, 'I know you love me, and you want to do things for me and protect me. But I love you too, and I want to do things for you and protect you. Give me that right!'

'Aye, I shall,' he said, kissing me, and then he laughed. 'Here's the pair of us, each protecting the other one from their own folk!'

We didn't have long together before I had to leave. I told him where I was going, and whom I was going to meet there. He didn't like it, but acknowledged that I was safe from Moore at the Rectory when it was full of people.

It wasn't that full when I arrived: I was one of the earliest. But more and more people arrived, and we were all soon enjoying ourselves. Caroline's head turned towards the door whenever it opened, but she was always disappointed: Robert Moore was not there.

About five in the afternoon, I noticed someone come in and speak quietly to Mr Helstone. He made an excuse and left hurriedly. The party went along merrily without him (rather merrier for his absence than his presence, in fact), and then he walked back in and announced baldly, 'Robert Moore has just been shot.'

Caroline fainted dead away. We all rushed round her with smelling salts and burnt feathers; gradually she began to come round.

I was angry with Mr Helstone, and I stalked over to him. 'How could you do that? How could you make that blunt announcement when Caroline was there?'

He looked at me in some surprise. 'Why? What's it to her?'

He didn't know. He really didn't know that his niece, with whom he lived all the time, whom he saw every day, whom he

178

was supposed to care for, felt anything other than common friendship towards Robert Moore. 'Anyway,' he added, 'it wasn't serious. Just a flesh wound in the thigh.'

'You hear that, Caroline?' I said, going over to her and patting her hand. 'Robert's all right. He's going to get better. He wasn't hurt much.'

Mr Helstone was surrounded by people asking him questions about the atrocity, and he was happy to oblige. 'It was about four o'clock. Moore was walking across the fields to come here. You know that grove of trees by the river? That's where it happened. There was nobody around, not a soul. Suddenly two men jumped out from the trees. One of them pulled a pistol out and shot Moore, then they ran away. Moore was dragging himself along trying to get here, when very fortunately a carter happened along and took him to the doctor, who patched him up.'

Then, in answer to more questions, he said, 'Yes, it was obviously Luddites: Moore saw the croppers' mark on their wrists. He managed to give an excellent description of the man who actually shot him. A very big man, late twenties, with blue eyes. And as they ran off, Moore heard the other man call him Tom.'

I greatly envied Caroline's ability to faint.

Could he have done it? Yes. He had everything necessary, including the knowledge that Moore would be on the road to the Rectory, because I'd told him.

Would he have done it? Yes. He had reasons a-plenty, from both Ludding and loving.

Did he do it? That I didn't know, and I fretted for days arguing one way or another.

It was the story of the other Luddite calling out 'Tom' that I didn't trust. If Samuel was any guide, his lads didn't call him anything, but simply referred to him as *him*, in a tone that implied that you would understand them because nobody else was worth talking about. And surely no Luddite would be so stupid as to call his name in such a conveniently incriminating way.

On the other hand, the brute fact remained: Robert Moore had been shot by *somebody*.

Then one morning when the letters arrived they included a poster, offering the sum of one thousand pounds to anyone who would give information leading to the apprehension and conviction of the villains who feloniously shot at and wounded Robert Moore, of Briarfield in the West Riding of the County of York, a clothier. There followed a horrifyingly detailed and accurate description of one of them, including the fact that his name was Tom.

At the bottom of the poster were scrawled the brief but wonderful words, *I didnt do it*.

Now I could act. I went straight down to the house by the mill where Moore lived with his sister Hortense, and was, I had been told, recovering from his wound. He didn't look to be recovering very well; there was a flush over his face that indicated fever. I disposed of Hortense with an excuse about wanting to talk about business. We were alone.

'The last time we met, Mr Moore, I told you to remember one very important fact; that you can go to the gallows for attempted rape and abduction of an heiress. You appear to have forgotten it.'

'Why do you think I could ever forget one second of that night, Shirley? What do you accuse me of?'

'You were attacked by some foolish Luddites with a grudge against you, and there's no shortage of those. You took your opportunity to have your revenge by putting the blame on to him and giving such an excellent description of him: including his name, which you overheard me say, and which no Luddite would be so incautious as to use in your hearing.'

'If you're right – and, mark, I don't say you are – what do you intend doing about it?'

'I intend to send you to the gallows if you don't retract. You could do it: you could claim to have been confused by the attack and made a mistake.'

'Of course I could. But I'm not going to. What if you do lay a charge against me? Who are your witnesses? You can hardly call your beloved Tom as one.'

'Sir Philip was there for much of the time. He'll bear me out.'

'You seriously think that he would be willing to stand up in open court and reveal his humiliation? He'd flee the country and never return rather than do that. Besides, in the unlikely event that you could get a conviction against me, the only effect would be to supply another motive for your beloved Tom. No, Shirley, I think I'm safe from your threat.' As I moved towards him with violence in my heart, and no doubt in my eyes, he added, 'And from threats of physical assault, too. You'll cherish me like a long lost son rather than make it the slightest bit more likely that your beloved Tom will face a charge of murder rather than the attempt at it. Now, go away and let me rest and recover. And just let me say before you go, that if I'm no man, a virago like you is no woman. Good afternoon, Miss Keeldar.'

He had me! The damned, loathsome, lying bugger had me! I went home and chopped a lot of wood, each log representing Robert Moore's head, and I used every word of the vocabulary I'd learned from Tom. Abraham silently tried to do it for me, but I told him I needed to smash something, and he went away in perfect understanding.

As the days passed, it seemed as though the bugger was going to die on me! The wound had become infected, and fever was spreading through his body. I plied Caroline with every medicine in the house and urged her to go and look after Robert at once. She couldn't have cared more about his safety than I did.

All attention was at the front of the house as a remarkably fine carriage drew up; outriders, postilion, everything. It was Earl Fitzwilliam. He was most civil, and suggested that we go and sit in the back garden together, where nobody could overhear us, as he wanted to have some private discussion with me.

'Your letter asking for mercy for the Luddites who attacked your mill,' he said as he produced it. 'I believe I may be able to accommodate you.'

'Oh, excellent, my lord,' I replied. 'Like you, I believe in stopping Luddism rather than persecuting Luddites.'

'I think we may have many beliefs in common, and that is why I am here to ask your help.'

'Which I shall certainly give: but I'm uncertain how. What have I to offer that other people cannot?'

'A good mind, a more compassionate approach than most of your fellow mill-owners, and most especially local knowledge. I'd like to put to you some of my ideas about suppressing Luddism in this area, and ask for your opinion on them.'

'Of course, my lord. I should be delighted.'

'We have had some success: there are now twelve other men in prison awaiting execution as well as the four you wrote of: in all, sixteen from this area. None of them has yet been hanged, and if I had my preference none of them would be. I believe in hanging as few men as possible.'

'I agree with you.' What was it about him? There was something in his tone that seemed to suggest an additional meaning lurking underneath the surface. I put it down to my natural suspicion of anyone with eyes as calculating as his, and attended to his words.

'Now, I have a little problem, and you may be able to help me solve it. I am asking you to draw on your experience with the Luddites. You have had more than your share, I believe.'

Oh, lots more, I thought. 'They attacked my mill.'

'And, of course, you have come face to face with their leader. I refer, naturally, to the time you so wisely refrained from shooting him and he behaved so chivalrously towards you.'

I was definitely suspicious of him now, and only nodded in agreement. I felt inclined to say as few words as possible; he would be on to my slightest slip.

'Let us consider his encounter with you. He had the courage to face your weapon, and the wit to know you wouldn't use it. The success of Luddite attacks in this area shows a formidable mind at work. He can inspire loyalty: one thousand pounds is a fortune for a working man or woman, and there must be hundreds of people who know where he is, but none has informed against him. All in all, I think we are looking at a remarkable man.' He paused, then added, 'You agree with me?'

I nodded again: my mouth was dry and I couldn't have said a word if I'd wanted to.

'A remarkable man: a dangerous man. Particularly since he now appears to have turned murderous.'

*He didn't do it!* I wanted to scream, but realized both how futile and how risky it would be to say so.

'Miss Keeldar, I said that there were sixteen Luddites awaiting execution. I also said I would prefer to hang as few as possible. In short, I would be happy to hang only one. Provided, of course, that it is the right one.'

I could not even nod, but sat motionless as he continued inexorably. 'Now, from your knowledge of this man – and you have met him in person – do you think that, if he knew that I would arrange to have the sentences on his sixteen men commuted to transportation, he might come forward and put his head in the noose to take their place?'

*Oh, he would, I know he would. He wouldn't hesitate for a second.*

'You think he would: I can see it in your face. Now we come to my little problem. He is not a fool, we have agreed on that. But he would be a fool to trust me. Miss Keeldar, you know that it wouldn't be in my interests to hang his men once I had him. Do you believe me – that I would keep my word and have the sentences on his men commuted? You don't give me an answer. I would appreciate one, if you would be so good.'

'Yes,' I whispered, because I did believe him.

'I am glad of that. Because you are the one who will convey my offer to him.'

'No!' I cried out with all my being. *Lord, let this cup pass from me*, I prayed. I made a desperate attempt to escape. 'Why do you think I have anything to do with this man?'

'Please don't attempt to deceive me. Someone must be very much more pickled in falsehood than you are to succeed at that. You may remember that I once warned you against being led astray by romantic fancy. I also told you that you were not foolish. I retract that statement.' He pulled another letter from his pocket, the one that I had written giving the Luddite demands, and put it next to the one asking for mercy. 'You really should have disguised your writing. Miss Keeldar, you have been very, very foolish.'

# PART 6

A man receiving his death sentence might need comforting embraces, or he might need to be alone, but what he does not need is a woman crying and demanding comfort from him.

What would be the best – the least dreadful – way of breaking it to him? *I have some very bad news.* No: he might even think it good news that he could save sixteen of his men. *I have some very serious news.* Yes. *I am the extremely unwilling bearer of –* No: he'd know I was extremely unwilling. *I have a message for you.* Keep it simple.

When I had the words right, I stood in front of the mirror practising them until I could say them without the slightest tremor of lip or blink of eye.

Then I made my preparations. Handkerchiefs: I'd try not to cry, but I took them anyway. Guards: I told them that they weren't needed since Moore was very ill. Mrs Pryor: I informed her that I didn't know when I was coming back and she was not to worry. Dress: the red one was perfect. One more rehearsal in front of the mirror, and I drove to Robin Hood's Tower for the last time.

'What's up, love? Tha looks like death,' he said as he helped me down from the cart.

I couldn't say it while looking at him so I stared at the tower as I came out with my speech.

'I have some very serious news. I received a visit from Earl Fitzwilliam. He has required me to pass on an offer to you. He will have the sentences of death on sixteen of your men commuted to transportation if you will hand yourself over to take their place.'

I'd said it without a tremor.

He seized me in his arms and held me. 'Oh, lass! My poor, poor lass. Having to say such a thing to me! Poor, brave lass.' He patted my head as if I were a child with a stomach ache. It was too much. I'd tried so hard to plan ways to comfort him, and now he was comforting me, and all my brave resolutions were gone as I sobbed bitterly in his arms.

'I'll kill the bugger for making thee say that. What did he do to thee? What did he threaten thee with?'

I could just speak now. 'Nothing. He simply pointed out that you'd never forgive me if I kept his offer from you.'

'Clever, clever bugger! There's nowt that I couldn't forgive thee, love, but I'd have to work hard on that one. But why choose thee? How does he know about us?'

'It was those letters: the one I wrote for that meeting and the one asking for mercy: he recognized the writing. And he chose me, because I believe him when he says he'll keep his word and commute the sentences, and you'll believe me.'

'Tha knows I'll take him up on it? Of course tha does, else tha wouldn't weep so hard.'

'Yes, I know. You're not afraid of death.'

'Nay, it's not death I fear. What frightens me is the thought of leaving thee. Of thee walking through life without me by thy side. Of not – not. . . .' I could feel him shaking, and a drop of moisture fell on me. 'Oh, damn it, it's unmanning me!'

He let me go, and rubbed his eyes and bit his lip trying to control it. 'Thanks, love,' he said as I silently passed him a handkerchief. He blew his nose. 'I like a lass that comes prepared.'

The smile he gave me was so brave that it set me crying again. 'Right pair of watering pots, aren't we?'

'I think we're allowed to be a bit upset in the circumstances.'

He didn't speak for a while, and I let him stay in his silence. Then he turned back to me, cupped my chin in his great hands, and looked down at my face. 'I love thee, and I know tha loves me. I'm going to ask thee to do summat for me that tha might not want to do. But I need thee to do it for me.'

I know what he's going to ask me, I thought. But I was wrong.

'I want thy word that when we part today, that's the end, and I'll not see thee again. Tha'll not come to my trial, nor stand by the gallows. Because I must show the buggers that I'm not one to weep and fall on my knees. And happen I'll not be able to do that if I see thee, or see a lass that I think might be thee. Tha saw me weeping, and I don't mind because it's thee. But I'll not have the bloody clothiers saying that I'm a coward. It's hard, what I'm asking thee, but tha loves me and tha'll do it for me.'

'I give you my word that when we part today you'll never see me again.'

'That's my lass!' he said, embracing me.

If he wasn't going to ask me, I'd have to ask him. 'I want you to do something for me, too.'

'Whatever tha wants.'

'Lie with me.'

He shook his head and smiled at me. 'Oh, nay, nay, love. I'll not ask thee to be brave and noble just because I must be.'

'You're not asking me: I'm asking you. And it has nothing to do with being brave and noble. It's because it's our last chance, and because we'll regret it the rest of our lives if we don't. And I'd like to point out that I'll have a lot longer to regret not doing it than you will.'

'But what if I get thee with child?'

189

'Don't you see that's one of the reasons I want to?'

'Tha's sure?'

'Yes. Do you want to?'

It was the only time that he held me so tightly that I couldn't breathe. 'Do I want to? Lass, that's the daftest thing I've ever heard thee say!'

'You'll have to show me what to do. I haven't done it before.'

'I know, love.' He let me go, stood me in front of him, held my arms and spoke to me intently. 'I know it's thy first time, and the first time should be a great and good and wonderful time. We've a deal of sorrow ahead of us, but let's try not to think about it, else it'll spoil it for thee. We'll remember it's thy first time, and forget it's my last. We'll laugh, and make jokes, and do daft things together. And the only future that we'll think on is the one when tha's old and grey and wrinkled, and tha's looking back on it, and tha's thinking, "That were grand! I'm glad I did that!"'

And now as I write this I am old and grey and wrinkled, and I am looking back on it, and I am thinking, 'That were grand! I'm glad I did that!'

'We've a choice here,' he said, looking around him. 'We can go over to them old ruins, and it'll be good and it'll be safe, or we can go to a place about four mile from here, and it'll be wonderful, but it'll be dangerous: we must go on the roads to get there and folk might see me.'

'Wonderful but dangerous sounds right for us, doesn't it?'

So he climbed into the back of the cart, and I threw a blanket over him, and once again he looked like a pile of old sacking. We didn't meet many people on the way, but Mr Helstone was one of them, and he asked my errand. *I'm off to give my virginity to General Ludd,* I thought, and as I told the rector some convenient lie, a warm wave of excitement flooded over me.

Following Tom's muffled directions, I pulled the cart up near the edge of a thick woodland. We let the horses roam in a field, picked up the blanket from the cart, and set off into the trees. As he carried me, I asked about the place.

'Lads and lasses have been coming here for thousands of years to do what we're going to do. Happen it's here that Robin Hood stopped Marian being a maid. And don't worry about anyone seeing us, because if anyone does, the only thing they'll think is that we got there before they did.'

I gasped with delight when we arrived. I have never seen a more beautiful place: in a clearing in the thick trees there were bluebells, and a little patch of grass rolled down to a stream. A clear fresh smell cut through the leaf-mould, and the rippling of the water merged with the calls of the woodland birds. It seemed designed for love-making: and if it was designed, then it had a designer, and that meant that God gave his blessing to us and did not think that it was a sin.

He set me down on my feet. Delicately he pulled the pins out of my hair and let it fall free, running the strands through his fingers and spreading it out over my shoulders. Those huge hands that I'd once thought so coarse brushed the back of my neck, and caressed my ears, and stroked my face, and his touch was as light as a summer breeze.

He spread the blanket out on the grass, then he took off his jacket and shirt, and rolled them into a ball to make a pillow. 'If I'd known we were going to do this, I'd have worn my silk-lined opera cloak.'

I made him stand still. 'When you were asleep in my bed recovering from your wounds, I looked at you, and I thought, *I'd like to stroke him*. I didn't do it then, so may I do it now?'

He opened his arms wide for me, smiling. I ran my hands over his great chest, combing the curls of hair with my fingers. I stroked the hard muscles of his arms and shoulders. 'I'm glad

191

tha didn't do that when I were asleep,' he said. 'It would have been a right waste.' I lifted his arm to my lips, and kissed the scar that had brought us together.

He put his hands to my dress, and began to undo the fastening. 'I like this dress,' he said. 'It's so easy to take off.'

'I know. That's why I chose to wear it today.'

'Wear this dress for me on the morning I go to the gallows, so I can spend my last hours imagining I'm taking it off thee. A man must have some fun before he dies.'

'And all morning I'll imagine you taking it off me. And when I read some pompous parson who's seen the blissful smile on your face saying, "Ah, he died in a state of blessedness," I can have a good laugh at him.'

'Let's laugh at all the buggers. Politicians, parsons, clothiers—'

'Mill-owners?'

'Not all mill-owners. It's grand, taking the clothes off a mill-owner's back, instead of the other way round.' I was naked by that time, and he stepped back and looked at me. 'Such a brave, true, beautiful mill-owner.'

He ran his hands over the curves of my body, fondling and admiring me, filling me with the aliveness of his touch that I'd first felt on Stilborough Moor, and I smiled as I recalled how horrified I'd been when I'd first dreamed of this.

Then he took his trousers off and I saw him naked. The size of him astonished me. I began to feel a little frightened. How was it going to fit in me?

'Don't be afraid, love. I'll not harm thee.'

'I know, but – the only naked men I've seen are Greek statues. And they're all small and curly things, not like that!'

He cupped my face in his hands. 'Happen it'll hurt thee a bit when I take thy maidenhead. Tha must tell me, and I'll stop. Tha must tell me if I do owt that hurts or displeases thee, and tha must tell me what pleases thee and what tha wants me to do.'

'And you must tell me.'

He made me lie on my back on the blanket, my head pillowed on his coat and shirt. The roughness of the cloth and the smell of his body from his clothes gladdened me, far more than silk sheets and soft perfume would have.

He lay beside me on the blanket, and he started to kiss me and stroke my body with his great hand. As his touch moved over me, caressing my breasts, my legs, my arms, I felt as though my flesh had become wax under the hand of a sculptor, and he was shaping me and smoothing me.

His hand came to rest between my legs, and I felt his touch explore my private parts: my no longer private parts. 'Does this please thee?'

'Oh, it pleases me.' For it was as if all the desire I'd ever felt for him was concentrated in just one place, where he was fondling me. 'Oh, yes, it *pleases* me.' I felt the excitement warm my body, and I gasped with bliss.

'Tha's ready for me, love,' he said, and he moved on top of me, taking his weight on his arms so he didn't crush me. My legs moved apart, and he lay between my thighs. I smiled up at him smiling down at me with the smile that had always warmed my heart, and he entered me.

There was a small burst of pain, and I must have winced at it, for he stopped moving. His eyes looked enquiringly at me, asking me what I wanted him to do. 'Don't stop,' I whispered, for although it had hurt a little, it seemed as though he had filled an emptiness in me that I hadn't known was there, and I couldn't bear to have him leave me. Then he was moving within me, hard and thrilling, and I closed my eyes, and we became one flesh.

Then he was moving harder, faster, and he gave a cry of

passion. It was over. A great wave of emptiness and desolation flooded through me as he left me. He lay by my side on the blanket, his hand cupping my breast.

'That was wonderful,' I whispered, wanting to please him, but he must have heard the catch in my voice.

'But much too fast,' he sighed.

'Mm.'

'I'm sorry, love, I truly am. I tried to last longer for thee, but the feel of thee, when it were what I've wanted for so long. . . .' He kissed me tenderly, and the emptiness and desolation left me. 'Never mind, we can stay here as long as we want to. It'll be better next time for thee, I promise. When this daft bugger has had time to recover. Look at him! He's had what he wanted, so he curls up and goes to sleep, never mind what thee and me want.' And indeed he did look much more like the small and curly Greek statues, only not so small.

'You mean it's as if you want to go one way, and your left foot decides to go another?'

'Summat like that. He's got a mind of his own, I know that.' He sat up slightly, resting his head on one hand, and smiled down at me. 'Dost tha recollect the night on Stilborough Moor?'

'Could I forget it?'

'Well, there's thee, waving thy pistol at me and threatening to shoot me any moment, and there's me, walking towards thee all brave and heroic like in front of the lads, wondering whether tha'll recognize me before tha shoots me or afterwards. And all the time I'm saying, "Down, boy, down. This isn't the time and place, and this isn't the lass for thee." Mind, I were right about the time and place, but he were right about the lass, so happen he isn't so daft after all. He knew it long before I did.'

'When did you know it?'

'When tha'd saved my life, and tha'd put me in thy bed, and tended me, and I fell asleep. And when I woke up, there tha were, lying beside me looking so beautiful and brave, and I knew then that for the rest of my life, if I woke up and tha weren't there, I'd miss thee and feel my arms were empty. So happen it's a good thing I'm getting hung – it'll save me a deal of bad mornings. When did tha know it were me?'

'When you picked up that chick and had to put it back in its nest.'

'Truly?' he said, surprised. I nodded. 'So I were doing my damnedest to be strong and brave showing off to thee, and all I needed to do was pick up a few gollins? I wish I'd known that. Would have saved me a deal of bother.'

He lay down again, flat on his back. and I snuggled up to him and rested my head on his shoulder and put my arm across his chest. I felt very relaxed and comfortable, and I'd had no sleep the night before, but I had to stay awake for him on his last day of freedom. I didn't want to waste an hour of it, so I mustn't let myself get too relaxed.

'Tha knows tha said I were to tell thee if there were owt I wanted?'

'Mm?'

'Happen it's not what tha thought of, love, but what I really want to do right now is to go to sleep with thee beside me, knowing that I'll wake up and tha'll still be beside me. Would tha mind?'

'I was trying to keep awake myself.'

He gave a rich, deep chuckle, leaned over and kissed me. 'Oh, lass, I love thee so much. Tha's got no regrets about what we've just done together?'

'My only regret is that we didn't do it earlier.'

I woke before him. I leaned up on my elbow, gently so as not to disturb him, so that I could study him.

He was snoring quietly. I didn't mind. I saw instead the scar on his arm from where he'd risked his life to save me, and another scar on his shoulder from where he'd done the same for one of his lads: he seemed to make a habit of saving people's lives. I saw the great muscles and sinews of his arms and chest and legs, and I smiled at the way he'd used their strength to show off to me when he hadn't needed to. I remembered his gentleness with the chick, and with me when he'd taken my maidenhead. I chuckled at the idea of him walking towards me and my pistol on Stilborough Moor, going 'Down, boy, down' – so that was what had caused the twinkle in his eye!

I thought of the way he laughed, and would find a joke, even a feeble one, to cover pain. And of the way he could think quickly in danger, and how we could each tell the other what to do with just a tiny gesture or a significant phrase. And of the way strong men spoke of him as though no one else was worth talking about, and of how there was not a soul in the area that would pick up a fortune and betray him.

All this would stop very soon at the end of a rope.

I couldn't thrust away that sort of idea on my own, so I tickled his ear. He gave a huge smile of delight as he woke up with me beside him as he'd longed to do. He pulled me into his arms, and for a long while we simply lay there together, not speaking, because we didn't need to.

'I'm concerned for thee, if tha's with child,' he said after a while. 'It's not a good life, being a fallen woman with a bairn and no husband.'

'I'll be a rich fallen woman. Money has its uses.'

He sat up straight. 'Happen I'll father a mill-owner. It's a fearful thought.' He pointed his finger just below my navel. 'Thee inside, it's thy dad talking. If tha must grow up to be a mill-owner, tha's to be one like thy mum. Tha's to have her beauty and my strength, and not the other way round. Hey, stop laughing, lass: tha's giving our child a rough ride, shaking thy belly like that.'

We went down to the stream to drink and to refresh ourselves, and I wiped away the stickiness between my legs with one of the handkerchiefs I'd brought to wipe away tears. Then he picked up the blanket, shook it and spread it out again for us, and we lay together for a while, stroking each other's bodies and saying silly things to each other.

'There's something I've never got round to telling you,' I said.

'Oh, aye: I hope it's not serious.'

'Well, I've been reading about hydrophobia, and d'you know something? Cauterizing the wound isn't the slightest bit of good. And in any case, dogs can be mad from things apart from hydrophobia.'

'Truly?'

'That's what this book said.'

'So the hot irons, and the fear hanging over us for months, happen they weren't needed? I'm glad I didn't know that!'

'Glad about it? When I think what I went through, when perhaps it wasn't necessary!'

'Aye, but we'd not have come together if it hadn't been for that, would we?'

'No, we wouldn't.' I laughed. 'We must be the only two people in the whole history of the world who've ever been glad they were bitten by a mad dog!'

He was erect, and we exchanged meaningful glances. I lay back on the blanket. 'Nay, love, tha goes on top this time. Tha'll not crush me like I'd crush thee.'

'But I don't know what to do.'

'Tha'll find out. And besides, tha mill-owner, tha'll not lay there in idleness with a poor man doing all the work.'

I sat astride him, and he smiled up at me. And suddenly I did know what to do. I pinioned his huge hands on the ground with my little ones, and he gave me his body to do with what I wanted. That great powerful body, that had always been so strong and protective, was *mine*.

It was me who made him sigh with delight as I let my hair fall down over him and brush his body. It was me touching him *here*, kissing him *there*, stroking him *this way*. It was my power, my desire, my control that caused him to writhe and gasp and groan. I could do it hard, I could do it softly, I could stop completely if I wanted to and make him beg, 'Go on, don't stop, please, please!'

It was my decision when to guide him into me, and fill the emptiness that yearned for him. It was the rhythm of my body that moved us, that sent the frenzy and passion surging through us, until it burst in an ecstasy that made us cry out together with the rapture of it.

I rested on him, feeling infinitely pleased with myself, and satisfied in every inch of my body. His arms enfolded me, and the rhythm of his breathing moved me gently. I understood what he had given me, out of his generosity and the greatness of his soul, and though I wouldn't have believed it possible, I loved him more than ever.

'Tha's got a gift of nature,' he said at last. 'If I hadn't taken thy maidenhead myself, I'd have thought tha'd been practising for years.'

'D'you know, I think you've just called me a whore?'

'Nay, nay, love. I wouldn't do that. Mind, when a man's going to die and he can't leave his fortune to his woman, it's a grand thing for him in his last hours to know that she'll always be able to earn her living.'

I pummelled his chest and rocked up and down with the laughter of his body. 'You should be repenting your sins in your last hours, Tom Mellor, and you've got more than your share of them.'

'Aye, lass. I'll say to the parson, "I lay with my love, and it were good. And, if you please, I'd much rather be doing it again with her than getting hung. And if I had my way, we'd do it again and again, year upon year, until we were both so old and stiff that we couldn't do any more than lie there and tickle each other." Happen he wouldn't believe me if I said I were repentant.'

I lay in his arms, and neither of us stirred. We both felt it, the knowledge that things could never get any better than this, and that the sad thoughts would soon start creeping in, and that it would be better for us to go now, while we were ahead. But neither of us could bear to leave.

He found the courage before I did. 'Let's go, love,' he sighed. So we washed ourselves, and dressed, and made sure that the place was just as beautiful for the next lad and lass as it had been for us.

He picked me up in his arms, took a step, then stopped. 'Did tha mean it, that tha really loved me because of that daft gollin?'

'Yes.'

'And I've no need to go on showing off to thee?'

'You never had.'

'Well, then, tha can walk.' He set me back on my feet. 'I'm fair worn out!'

I stayed a moment looking back. I thought of all the other lads and lasses who'd done the same as we had for thousands of years. I wondered if some of the lasses had done it for the same reason as I had. It pleased me to imagine some Brigante maiden, blushing shyly in her woad, offering herself to her hairy warrior before he went off to fight the Romans. It pleased me to think of all the lasses and lads to come afterwards for thousands of years, and I hoped they'd find as much delight there as we'd done.

I'm glad that I didn't know then that we were among the last to go there. The trees have been chopped down to make way for mills and houses, and the stream is thick with filth. No more lads and lasses will come to take joy in each other's bodies in that beautiful and private place in the bluebell wood.

He stood by me as I sat in the cart ready to go, holding my hand for the last time. There were so many things we could have said to each other, but we didn't, because we each knew that the other knew them already.

'Farewell, lass,' he said, and let go my hand.

'Farewell, lad,' I said, and I picked up the reins. 'Remember, let's laugh at the buggers.'

'Aye, let's laugh at 'em.'

I drove away, without a tear in my eye, and I didn't look back.

And I did laugh at the buggers when they rejoiced at the capture of General Ludd himself, Thomas Mellor.

And I laughed at them when they fumed about the leniency of Earl Fitzwilliam in having the death sentences on sixteen Luddites commuted to transportation.

And when Robert Moore recovered, and smiled at me in such a way that I knew he was gloating at me, I thought of Tom's hands squeezing his private parts and his throat, and I laughed at him, too.

And the only time I cried, great sobs of inconsolable loss that went on for hour after hour, was the day I discovered that I was not carrying Tom's child.

Robert Moore proposed to Caroline Helstone, and was accepted. After the wound to his pride at the hand of a virago, and the wound to more than his pride at the hand of the virago's lover, a soft, gentle hand soothing his fevered brow must have been irresistible.

So here we were celebrating, three days after Thomas Mellor, cropper, of the West Riding of Yorkshire, had been sentenced to death for the attempted murder of Robert Moore, clothier, also of the West Riding, and three days before his execution for that heinous crime. I was almost certain that Moore had fixed the date of his wedding deliberately to fall then. Whether it was deliberate or not, he must have relished the sight of me as a bridesmaid to his radiant bride.

She was radiant, of course: as radiant as only a woman can be who has loved a man so long and so deeply and so hopelessly, and who then finds herself loved by him in return. I was willing to believe that he did love her: she was a lovable woman, and I'd never thought him incapable of seeing merit.

The bridal pair were mingling with the guests at the wedding breakfast, and I was chatting to Mr Helstone when Robert Moore came up to me.

'I must apologize for intruding business on such a day, but I wonder if I may speak with you, Miss Keeldar. We so rarely see each other these days.'

'It's your wedding, Mr Moore. What would you like to discuss?'

We made an apology to Mr Helstone, and moved through the crowd, discussing business. Yes, reader, he was still my tenant. I confess that one night I had written a letter to my lawyer, telling him to evict Moore and find someone else. Overnight I thought of the two hundred jobs in the mill, and of the fact that, whatever I felt about him, Moore was almost certainly a better employer than any who would replace him. I tore the letter up, revolted at the idea that I had so nearly carried out my revenge on two hundred innocent people, just because I had the power to. After that, I just laughed every time I received my rent and the repayment of my loan, fancying how he must have hated to pay.

By this time I was good at laughing at the buggers. I laughed at the hanging judge who had presided over Tom's trial, and at the jury, packed with property owners, that had convicted him. I knew that most of the evidence on both sides was out-and-out perjury – there must have been hundreds of people willing to lie to give Tom an alibi, though only six had done so.

Moore and I reached a quiet spot in the garden where we could not be overheard. 'You can dispense with your guards now, Shirley,' he said. 'I'm satisfied with my revenge. Or at least I shall be at noon in three days' time when I stand in the crowd at York and watch him hang.'

'I would recommend, Mr Moore, that if you have a regard for your safety, you choose a spot well away from any croppers,' I replied coolly, laughing inwardly at the way he was trying to goad me. My defences were far too strong to let this sort of gloating bother me.

'I did enjoy the trial,' he continued. 'Watching your beloved Tom looking so brave, and knowing that he would hang because of what I said.'

I was sure that Tom had thought of something to make him laugh at Moore, and I wondered what it was, and I smiled.

'I was curious to see whether you would be called to give him an alibi,' he continued. 'I'd always hoped that you were with him at the time, and would come forth to sacrifice your honour to admit it and save him.'

'You should have remembered that I was at Caroline's party that afternoon,' I said, smiling at the thought that, if I hadn't been there in front of dozens of witnesses, I would have been delighted to swear that Tom was with me whether or not it was true.

'Yes, I should. Then I'd have picked a better time.'

'How could you have picked a better time to be shot? Oh!' I stopped smiling, which was doubtless his intention in saying it.

'Yes, Shirley. There never were any Luddites.'

'You shot yourself?' He nodded. 'But you nearly died!'

'Yes, I didn't take the fever into account. But I don't regret that. I gained a soft, sweet-tempered, adoring, submissive wife out of it. A woman, in fact.'

*Laugh at the bugger, laugh.* But I was hard pressed to find something to laugh at. He knew that he was safe in telling me, for who could I tell? Who would believe me, when all he'd have to do was reveal that Tom was my lover? Then I recalled my favourite thought about Moore, and I knew that when he had been testifying, Tom too would have laughed at the thought of squeezing private parts, and I recalled that this was Moore's wedding night, and I smiled.

'Caroline is far too good for you, and I hope one day you'll realize it. Good day, Mr Moore.'

The next day I bade farewell to Samuel and Abraham. 'Will you be able to get work?' I asked.

'Aye,' said Samuel. 'There's always work for strong men.' He sighed. 'But not in cropping any more.'

No. There wouldn't be. Despite all the love I felt for their leader, I always knew that the Luddites would lose. I'd seen the sums, I'd heard the arguments, I'd examined the frames. The machines would take over from those strong, skilled men, and the most they could do was fight a delaying action.

'Happen you saved our skins when you made us get untwisted,' he went on. 'So we're right grateful.'

I probably had. Sooner or later these two would have been caught or killed, and at best there would have been eighteen rather than sixteen who were sentenced to transportation rather than the gallows.

'We lost. But it were worth the fight, weren't it?'

I thought of all the dead men, on both sides. Of the families torn apart by transportation. Of the smashed frames, smashed bones, smashed lives.

Then I thought: sometimes it's better to smash something. Sometimes you have to pick up your Enoch. Because if you don't, if you just take everything lying down, you end up like fawning, servile Johnnie.

'I don't know, Samuel. I really don't know.'

'He thought it were worth it.'

'Yes, he did.' We were talking of him in the past tense, though he was still living and breathing.

'You were his woman, weren't you?'

I wondered how long they'd known, and how they'd found out. No point in denying it now. 'Yes, I was.'

'We're right pleased he had you to gladden his days. Mind, if we'd heard about it before we knew you, we'd have thought he were betraying us, and it would have broken our hearts.'

So even now he could surprise me into loving him more: I hadn't realized exactly what he'd risked by loving me. 'You won't tell anyone else, will you?' I asked. 'He wouldn't like it.'

'Nay, we won't. You'll be going to see him off, then?'

'No. He made me give my word that I wouldn't.'

'Happen he were right. But we'll go, and we'll think of you.'

'Thank you, Samuel. For all you've done for me. And you, too, Abraham.'

Then Abraham, the man who never spoke two words in a day if he could help it, reached out his strong, delicate cropper's hands, took mine and patted them. 'We're right sorry for you, lady,' he said.

This unexpected sympathy broke through my defences, and my eyes started to water. They saw, they understood, and they left.

It was five o'clock in the morning. He had seven more hours to live. I was glad now that he'd made me promise not to stand by the scaffold: it would have been as unbearable for me as it would have been for him.

Suddenly there was a knock on my door: it was Mrs Pryor.

'Shirley, will you come downstairs? It's Caroline, and she's in trouble and needs your advice.'

For a moment I was tempted to refuse my help: God knows I had troubles enough of my own. But that would have been unkind: why should I take my misery out on others? I donned my red dress – it was easy to put on. I'd laid it out the night before, ready to wear for him on his last morning.

Why was Caroline here at this ungodly hour? She was wringing a handkerchief between her hands, and looked as though she'd just used it to wipe away a tear. Only three days married, and she looked like this.

'I just don't know what to do, Shirley. I couldn't sleep, so I came to ask Mamma's advice, and she says I must do it, but it's probably too late now anyway. What do you think?'

Mrs Pryor came to her aid. 'It's Robert Moore,' she said. 'Yesterday he went to York, to see that Luddite executed today. He was in very good humour, and Caroline asked him why. So he told her. . . .'

He'd told her!

He hadn't told her the reason, of course: he'd said he'd done it to ensure that the Luddite leader was executed. He'd seen the adoration in his wife, but he hadn't seen the integrity. The only thing that stopped me laughing uproariously at the bugger's folly was the sight of her in front of me, torn apart between her love and her knowledge that an innocent man should not hang.

'So what do you think I should do? Mamma says that I must report what Robert told me, but how can I? In any case, whom do I report it to and how could I do it in time to stop the execution?'

'If you decide you must go I shall be delighted to drive you to York,' I said, remarkably calmly. I'd nearly refused to listen to her! 'Earl Fitzwilliam is there, and he has the power to stop it. It is almost half past five: the execution is at noon: the journey will take about six hours. Your decision, whatever it is, must be made immediately. Now, I shall have the cart made ready and prepare for our journey. I shall drive round to the front, and then you will come out, and you will tell me whether to drive you to York or back home. Meanwhile, I suggest that you listen to the words of your wise and kind mother.'

*And if they don't work*, I thought as I rushed out, woke Johnnie to help me get the cart ready, and grabbed everything I would need, especially a watch, *I'll try kidnapping*.

Mrs Pryor ushered Caroline out to me as I waited in the cart, and helped her climb up. 'Which is it to be? York or home?'

'Oh, I know that I should stop the execution. But I swore to love, honour and obey Robert only three days ago. What would you do, Shirley, if you loved a man like I love Robert?'

'Caroline, your husband has committed perjury. That is a crime, but he may escape punishment so long as there is no serious consequence. But if a man hangs as a result of it, then he will have committed murder. And that is a capital offence,' I said, then took her hand. 'Believe me, if I loved a man as you love Robert, I would do anything to save him from the gallows. And that includes risking his anger because I've broken my word to him.'

'Shirley, you're right. Quick, we must go to York as fast as we can, to save Robert!'

'God speed you, both my daughters,' Mrs Pryor called as we drove out. 'Go and save the man you love, Caroline!' And as we left, I heard her add, 'You too, Shirley.'

Good heavens! I thought as I realized what she'd meant. How did she find out? And how many more people know of my love? I must be getting as transparent as Caroline.

My cart and my good horses were chosen to go well over the horrible moorland roads, and I drove as fast as compatible with safety, and usually faster. There wasn't much light as we started, but I and the horses knew the road for the first part of the journey until the sun was fully risen. I was feverishly trying to do calculations in my head: if I went *this* way, it'd be longer, but more of it would be on good road; on the other hand, *that* way was shorter in miles, but was it shorter in time? Should I change horses in one of the towns on our way to the main road? It'd mean fresh horses, but it would take time, and they wouldn't be as good as my own excellent pair. All the while, I feared that he might die because of my poor arithmetic.

We came to a fork in the road; I made my decision; and that was it.

After that, I could spend time reassuring Caroline that she was doing the right thing: not only for the sake of justice, but for Robert's as well. I thought of the effect she would make on Earl Fitzwilliam. He wouldn't believe me if I told him the story; he knew I'd lie through my teeth to save my man: yes, and practise hard enough to be convincing. But Caroline, so stammering, so reluctant to reveal the truth – oh, he'd believe her.

I realized as she spoke of her fears and doubts that it was not a simple conflict between love and justice that tore her apart. What Robert had told her had changed her love for him.

I wondered what I would do if I were in her position. It was easy for me to choose my man over the law; when I'd rescued him from the militia, the only question in my mind was how, not whether, to do it. He had done plenty of wrong things, plenty of illegal things, but as far as I knew he'd never done any despicable things. He'd never done anything that lowered him in my mind, that lessened my love for him. I believed he never would – but no doubt Caroline had believed that too.

No thought of her own future crossed her mind. I resolved that if Moore threw her out, as was quite possible, I'd divide my income equally with her to ensure her financial comfort if nothing else. Then I'd have to tell her that I had my own reason for wanting to stop the execution or she wouldn't accept it, but unless that happened I would keep to the part of disinterested helper. She had conflict enough without asking her to weigh her inevitable horror at my choice of man against the ties of our friendship.

We reached the main road. We needed to go at least nine miles an hour from now on, and there was no way my tired horses could do that. I'd decided not to change them, preferring them to strange horses over the country roads. But now I needed something faster, much faster. Unfortunately, there was not a sign of a changing post. I was silently screaming in vexation as I urged them, painfully slowly, along the road to York.

Then one of them went lame.

*A horse! A horse! My mill for a horse!* I wanted to cry out, as I jumped down from the cart and inspected the hoof. I am not one of those ladies who can shoe her own horses, but I could see that the foot was swollen. I bit my lip, wondering whether it would be faster to cut the horse loose, re-rig the cart, and drive on with only one, or to keep the lame horse going until we reached somewhere that it could be replaced.

'We aren't going to get there in time, are we?' asked Caroline, her face filled with frustration and terror, as I realized mine must be.

Then, from back along the road behind us, we heard the most musical sound I have ever heard in my life. A horn, the wonderful horn of the Royal Mail coach to York, warning other vehicles to get out of the way.

'What are you doing?' Caroline asked me as I pulled the cart and horses across the road to block it. 'We can't stop the Mail: it's a crime.'

'It's the fastest thing on the road.'

'We *can* stop the Mail,' she said, jumping out and joining me in waving frantically for it to stop.

The mail coach pulled to a halt, the horses rearing up before our faces, the coachman swearing at us. But it is difficult for any man to get seriously angry at a pretty damsel in distress, and there were two of us.

'Help us!' I cried. 'A man's life is at stake. We must get to York as soon as possible. Please take us up with you.'

'No room. Now get that cart out of the way!' shouted the coachman.

I called out to the passengers. 'Here's my cart and two fine horses. They belong to the first two people who'll give up their places to us.'

'That's us!' cried a voice from inside, and a fat merchant and his fatter wife jumped nimbly out of the coach before anyone else could take up the offer. We thanked them profusely but very quickly as we climbed into the coach. The merchant pulled the cart out of the road, and we were off.

We slumped together in relief. Our two fellow inside passengers were clearly travelling companions: both about forty, they had *clothier* written all over them.

'Excuse me,' I asked one of them. 'What time is the Mail due in at York?'

'A quarter before twelve,' he said. 'Though we might be late because of the delay that you young ladies have caused us.'

Caroline and I stared at each other. Fifteen minutes at most to get out of the coach at York, to get to the castle where the hanging would take place, to reach Earl Fitzwilliam, to explain everything, and for him to stop the execution. Could it be done? Well, it would have to be, and there was no way we could get there any faster.

We were both exhausted. Neither of us had had any sleep, and the agony of frustration beside a lame horse had ruined our nerves. We were lucky that it had been inside passengers that had first accepted my offer. The outside passengers, in their cheaper seats, would have a rougher ride than we would.

'Caroline,' I said, holding her hand, and trying to convince myself as much as her. 'We're on one of the fastest coaches in England. If anything can get us there in time, it's this. We must bless the chance that our horse went lame and drove us in desperation to stop the Mail. Now we can do nothing but rest and save our energy for when we get there.'

Our fellow passengers were staring at us curiously, but I did not expect much sympathy from them, and I did not feel like explaining ourselves. They resumed their interrupted conversation.

It soon became clear that they were talking about the obvious item of news for any clothier going to York that day: the hanging of that notorious Luddite Thomas Mellor. They were both united in condemnation of the Luddites, and in their approval of the death penalty for frame breaking. But it seemed to me that one of them, a thin gaunt man, was reluctant to give his approval to the execution that was to take place. He was a fraction less bloodthirsty than his companion, who said, 'I'd hang the lot of them. And in my view, it's a damned shame that he's the only one on the scaffold today.'

'If it was any other of the vermin, I'd agree with everything you say,' said the gaunt man. 'But Tom Mellor saved my life once, and I'm sorry I shan't have the chance to return the favour.'

My God, another one! I thought. How many of us are there who owe our lives to him? This was an opportunity too good to waste.

'Excuse my interruption, sir, but you may still have the chance to do so. We've information that proves Tom Mellor is innocent, and we must get there in time to stop the execution. If you can think of any possible way in which you can help us—'

He didn't hesitate. He leaned his head out of the window and shouted up to the coachman, 'There's a guinea in it for you for every minute you shave off the time we arrive at York!'

'I'm sorry, sir, I'm going as fast as I can. We're fully laden.'

'What's up?' we heard one of the outside passengers say. 'Did I hear you say summat about stopping Tom Mellor hanging?'

'That's right,' said the gaunt man. 'These two young ladies are trying to get there in time.'

'Well,' said the outside man. 'If it'll lighten the load and get the lasses there faster, happen I don't need this.' We heard the sound of a box falling off the roof. 'And I don't need this.' Another box fell. 'And happen I don't need to get to York today that much myself.' And we saw him launch himself off the coach and tumble into the road.

Then there was a flurry of boxes falling into the road, as other passengers in the cheap seats – the poorer people – threw their belongings off the coach to save Tom Mellor's life. None was so brave as to follow the first man's example and launch themselves from a fast coach, but they all climbed off at the first stop we came to, and prevented anyone else taking their place. And the ostlers worked even faster than they normally did, and the coachman took risks that he wouldn't normally do, and he pulled up quite illegally at the road that led to the castle to set us down.

At half past eleven.

The gaunt man threw fifteen guineas to the coachman and jumped down with us. 'I'll clear the way for you,' he said, and we ran behind him.

The scaffold was set up between the assize court and the bailey wall. There was nobody on it yet, but a troop of soldiers stood round it, guarding it from the largest crowd of people I have ever seen. Oh, God! I thought. The dreadful irony if we are prevented from saving him by the sheer number of people who've come here to show their support for him.

'We must get through!' cried the gaunt man as he tried to push forward. But people wouldn't get out of the way fast enough.

Suddenly there was an exclamation. 'Caroline!' came the voice of Robert Moore, as he elbowed his way towards us.

I didn't expect her resolution to last two seconds in his presence. I looked around at the faces that had turned towards us, and found what I was searching for: big men with croppers' marks on their wrists.

'Help us!' I shouted to them. 'We have information that will save Tom Mellor's life if we can get it to Earl Fitzwilliam in time. And that man' – I pointed to Moore as he stood aghast – 'is trying to stop us.'

A wall of croppers appeared between Moore and us. A phalanx of burly men formed around us and arrowed its way through the crowd. 'Up here!' cried the gaunt man, who was still with us and knew the way.

The croppers followed the clothier's lead, ran up the stairs, and brushed aside the soldiers who stood in their way. They burst open a door, and there, rising from his seat in astonishment, was Earl Fitzwilliam.

'My lord!' I cried. 'We must speak to you. Tom Mellor is innocent. Tell him your story, Caroline.'

She looked around. 'Not in front of all these people,' she said. I could see her point: the croppers would have killed her husband if they'd heard what she had to say.

I quickly shooed everyone out. 'Thank you, thank you all. And pray that we are in time.'

'Miss Keeldar, Miss Helstone, please inform me of the reason for this interruption,' said Earl Fitzwilliam.

'It's not Miss Helstone, it's Mrs Moore now,' I said. 'And that's the point. Tell him.'

She let her story out, slowly and reluctantly; and though I

knew that every hesitation only made her more believable, I could have screamed with frustration at the way she stammered and stumbled.

I looked out of the window. Oh, God, he was being brought on to the scaffold. A black hood was placed over his head, and the prison chaplain was speaking to him. The hangman stood beside him, ready to do his work. I could hear the enormous crowd join in the hymn:

> *'Behold the Saviour of Mankind*
> *Nailed to the shameful tree*
> *How vast the love that Him inclined*
> *To bleed and die for me.'*

I knew what he was thinking of inside the black hood: he was taking the red dress off me. If I failed, he wouldn't know I was here wearing it. Only if I succeeded in having that hood taken off him would he see me again, and I'd have broken my word to him.

'Mrs Moore,' said Earl Fitzwilliam as Caroline finished. 'I must think about the implications of your story. And I must, of course, see your husband before I make any decision.'

'My lord, there isn't time!' I cried in agony. 'He's on the scaffold right now.'

'Very well, I see the urgency.' He summoned a soldier. 'See if you can find Mr Robert Moore in that crowd. Take Mrs Moore with you: she will help you to identify him. Bring them both back here as soon as you can.'

Then he leaned out of the window and shouted, 'Stop the execution!' Nobody took any notice. Nobody could hear him above the singing. Nobody looked at him as he tried to catch the hangman's attention but failed.

'This is most unfortunate,' he said. He sent a soldier to run as fast as he could, but would he be fast enough? 'Miss Keeldar, will you assist me in attracting the hangman's attention? What are you doing? This is hardly the time to disrobe.'

Thank God it's so easy to take off, I thought, as I leaned out of the window, waving my dress like a red flag.

'Can you think of anything better to attract a man's attention than a young woman in a petticoat?'

'A young woman out of a petticoat?' he suggested mildly.

'If it's necessary.' But it wasn't. I could see faces in the crowd turning to us, and hands pointing to us. I could hear the hymn die down as people stopped singing. Then, at last, someone made the hangman look up at us.

Earl Fitzwilliam leaned out of the window and bellowed, 'Stop the execution!'

There was a giant roar of approval from thousands of throats, echoing and billowing through the air. The hangman reached out and pulled the hood off Tom's head. I could see him shake his head in the light, then look around him to the thousands of faces, and then up to where everyone was pointing, up to the window, where I was in my petticoat with my red dress in my hand.

His legs buckled and he fell to his knees.

'After that somewhat melodramatic event,' said Earl Fitzwilliam, as I put my dress back on, 'I think that a dish of tea would be an advisable and welcome anticlimax.'

He ordered some, and we sat and drank it together and discussed the weather. I realized that he might be a cynical, shrewd, calculating old man, but he was not naturally a cruel one, and he knew that I needed something utterly prosaic to restore my nerves. He was prepared to be cruel if it was in his interests, as it had been when he'd forced me to convey his offer to Tom, but there was a streak of compassion there as well.

Our discussion of the merits of Dr Johnson's dictionary was interrupted at length by the arrival of Caroline and Robert Moore. Her face was ghastly white; his was red with anger.

'I shall never, ever forgive you for this,' he said to her.

'Ah, Mrs Moore, Mr Moore,' said Earl Fitzwilliam. 'Pray join us in a dish of tea. Will you pour, Miss Keeldar?'

Moore shot me a glance of such loathing that I felt it should have curdled the milk. I was glad of it: the more hatred he felt for me, the less he'd feel for Caroline.

'Mr Moore,' continued Earl Fitzwilliam. 'I couldn't help but overhear your remark to your wife. I rather think that you should be going down on your knees and thanking her with all your heart for what she has done today for you.'

'What?' cried Moore. 'I trusted her, and she betrayed me!'

'On the contrary. She has saved your life. If Mellor had died today on your word, you would have followed him to the gallows within a very short space of time after I had found out what you had done. And I would have done, Mr Moore. Believe me, I would have done. I was always suspicious of that convenient fellow who called out his name. It was not in my interests to investigate any further: we were going to hang him for something in any case. But perjury and murder will out in the end, and sooner or later I would have discovered the truth. There are very few people in this world who can get the better of me, and you are not one of them.'

Moore's face was a picture of conflicting emotions as he weighed Earl Fitzwilliam's words.

'I shall not charge you with perjury,' Earl Fitzwilliam continued. 'It would not be in my interests to reveal how you have behaved. However, I should certainly have charged you with murder if your wife had not saved you. Mrs Moore,' he continued, 'I know how difficult it has been today for you. My admiration for your resolution is unbounded. Not one woman

215

in a thousand would have shown such integrity as you have, nor such clear-sighted affection, that can see what is needed rather than what is wanted. Your husband may take a little time to see the truth about you, and to understand what an extraordinarily lucky man he is in gaining your love. I heard him say that he would never forgive you. Because you love him, despite what he has done, I hope you will be able to forgive him.'

As I saw the effect of his words on Caroline, how the blood came back to her cheeks and the torment faded, I forgave him for what he had done to me. Cynically, shrewdly and calculatingly he was giving Caroline the only reward she wanted for informing on her husband: the belief that she had saved him by doing so.

Whether her husband believed the same was a different question. But at least he no longer looked at her with fury. He did not pull away his hand as she timidly reached for it.

'Mr Moore, may I suggest that, as you take your excellent wife home, you reflect on what I have said? And consider: unquestioning devotion is a fine quality in a dog; in a wife, integrity is rather more important.' He ushered the pair to the door. 'Mrs Moore, if I am ever in any position to serve you, you have only to ask.' Then, as they left, he called to one of the soldiers, 'Fetch the man Mellor up here.'

He closed the door, saying, 'Well, I hope that works.'

'It may do. He does love her.'

He paced a little round the room, looking perturbed. 'Miss Keeldar, it is with considerable regret that I must tell you this. I have given Mrs Moore the belief that she has saved the man she loves. It greatly grieves me that I can give no such comfort to you.'

'What? But he's innocent!' I cried, horrified.

'Of the attempted murder of Mr Moore, certainly. But he is guilty of half a dozen other capital crimes. I am afraid that all you have done today is put off the moment. I am sure that he knows it himself. I wish that you had known it too.'

He turned away to allow me time to struggle with myself. The pain of it was as bad as the time I had delivered Tom's death sentence. No, worse: for then I had been forced into it. This time, of my own free choice, I had broken my word to him, and made him fall to his knees in front of thousands, and all for nothing!

'Perhaps it would have been better if I had let the execution go ahead,' he said at length. 'But I do have a heart, and the pleas of two such women as you and Mrs Moore moved it before I could reflect clearly.'

The door opened, and there he was, hands manacled behind his back, with a soldier each side of him. We looked at each other; he winked at me; and we each knew what the other wanted to say.

*Forgive me, Tom.*

*There's nowt that I couldn't forgive thee, love.*

'Unlock his hands, and leave us,' Earl Fitzwilliam said to the soldiers. They looked doubtful. 'Stand guard outside the door – there are plenty of armed men outside to stop him escaping through the window.' They obeyed and left the three of us alone.

'You're a brave man, I'll say that for you,' Tom said. 'I could kill you with my bare hands before them guards had a chance to stop me. I've nowt to lose. You didn't hang me today, but you'll hang me some time.'

'I'd be a brave man only if you were a stupid one, Mellor. But you know that if you killed me, you would unleash on your people a wave of repression that would make me seem as mild in comparison as Miss Keeldar.'

'Aye, happen it would. And happen that'd make every poor man and woman in England finally see you and yours for what you are, and they'd take up arms and fight you, and heads would go under the guillotine.'

'Perhaps you're right: perhaps you're wrong. You won't risk it. You don't have the ruthlessness to start a revolution. I knew it when you put your head in the noose to save your men. You would have done your cause far more good if you'd stayed free and let them hang. Compassion is an admirable quality, Mellor, but not when taking on the English ruling classes.'

Tom sighed in defeat. 'Nay, I'll not kill you.'

'Now, because I can afford to show compassion even though you can't,' Earl Fitzwilliam continued, 'I'll leave you alone with Miss Keeldar for five minutes before I send the soldiers in to take you away.' He turned to me and said, 'Miss Keeldar, you have my most sincere and profound sympathy. Even a romantic fancy can hurt. I hope that one day you will find a gentleman who can take away the pain you feel today.'

Then all the feelings, all the beliefs I'd held back and controlled for so long burst through me, and I had to speak.

'You talk to me of finding a gentleman? I've seen gentlemen! One would have raped me, another ran away and left me to be raped. I found something much better: I found a man. I've seen him lift two big croppers and throw them out the door; I've seen him care for a little chick that had fallen out of its nest. He saved my life: not because he loved me – anyone with any courage would wish to do that. But I was a stranger to him then, and he risked a horrible death for me.

'You may not listen to me because you think I have some romantic fancy for him. But listen to the voices of the thousands of people who rejoiced today when the execution was stopped. We arrived here in time to stop it because poor people threw their belongings off the coach to lessen the load and speed us up. And because a clothier abandoned all his opinions to help us save the life of someone who'd once saved his.

'I know this man. I've laughed with him, yes, and I've lain with him. Don't you dare tell me that what I feel for him is a romantic fancy. And know this, my lord, that when you hang him, you will be hanging a far, far better man than you.'

I was panting, and I could feel my face flushed with passion.

'I shouldn't do this,' Earl Fitzwilliam sighed. 'At my age I ought to have more self-control. But I shall, on this one occasion, put my desires before my reason. Miss Keeldar, you may count yourself among the handful of people who have ever beaten me. His sentence will be commuted to transportation for the term of his natural life.'

The relief that flooded through me stopped me speaking for a moment, but eventually I managed to express my immense gratitude.

'I suppose it would be too much to expect you to express any gratitude, Mellor.'

'Aye, it would. Happen I should, because you've pleased her. But I can't feel it for myself. Do you know what you've sentenced me to? A lifetime of waking up without her beside me. Of knowing, every minute of every day of every year for the term of my natural life, that there's the width of the world between us. You know what she is: you've seen her and she's reached your heart. Think what she is to me, when I've held her arms in mine, when I've felt her body next to mine, when I've touched her lips with mine. I'll take your offer of transportation, but only to save her pain. If it were my choice alone, I'd ask you to send me back to the gallows.'

'I don't see the necessity of the choice.'

'What?'

'Miss Keeldar, allow me to give you some information of which you may be unaware. The penal colony of New South Wales desires to attract free settlers of fortune. It offers many inducements, including the possibility of having convicts assigned as labour. Now, if a single young woman were to ask me whether she should go out there, I should strongly advise her against it: the difficulties and hardships would be far too great for her. Unless, that is, she had immense courage and determination. And unless she could be assured of finding among the convicts a foreman she could trust to be her right-hand man. He would have to be a natural leader, of course, one with great strength in both mind and body. Such men are rare. I shall bid you farewell now. As I said: the soldiers will be here in five minutes to take him away.'

Then this improbable Cupid left us alone. It took us a few seconds to realize that he had offered us something we'd never had before: a future together.

'Can I ask thee, love?'

'You've no need to ask.'

'It'll be hard.'

'Harder than parting?'

'Happen not.'

We wasted no more time in talking: we had only a few minutes before the soldiers came in. Our kiss had to last us until we could kiss again, on the other side of the world.

Reader, I married him. That's all I need tell you about this part of our story. Perhaps later I shall write about what happened afterwards: about the hardships we faced – bad enough for me, a free settler, but hell for him, a convict, until the day he gained his ticket of leave.

I could write of the problems of changing from Miss Keeldar the heiress to Mrs Mellor the convict's wife. And the towering arguments, for two strong-willed people do not always live together in perfect harmony. And the partings: he could never return to England and I sometimes had to, and I saw the mills and houses spread over the land, and the fog of Victorian respectability settle on the country like a shroud.

I'd tell of the struggle he had to keep faith with his principles, difficult when he was a convict, but even more difficult after he became rich in his own right, in a colony that depended on labour forced from the convicts and land forced from the Aborigines.

I could include the stories of the men and women who took up the fight after him, like the Tolpuddle Martyrs and the Chartists. We knew many of them, those who escaped the gallows and arrived in chains: they were the best that England sent out.

Above all, I'll tell of the laughter and joy we shared, and of our children and grandchildren, and the little girl who sat on her great-grandfather's lap and demanded a story about Enoch the friendly hammer.

Yes, I shall carry on writing. For writing this has helped in a small way to fill the huge, gaping hole in my life since the night that he fell asleep with me beside him, and he didn't wake up.

# Resources

**Luddism, especially in the West Riding**
Bailey, Brian, *The Luddite Rebellion* (Sutton Publishing, 1998)
Bull, Angela, *The Machine Breakers: The story of the Luddites* (William Collins, 1980)
Greanleaf, E.P. and Hargreaves, J.A., *The Luddites of West Yorkshire* (Kirklees Cultural and Leisure Services, 1986)
Kipling, L. and Hall, N., *On the Trail of the Luddites* (Pennine Heritage Network)
Sale, Kirkpatrick, *Rebels against the Future* (Addison-Wesley, Reading, Mass., 1996)
Thomis, Malcolm I., *The Luddites: Machine-breaking in Regency England* (Gregg Revivals, 1993)
Thompson, E.P., *The Making of the English Working Class* (Penguin, 1991)

**Literature**
Brontë, Charlotte, *Jane Eyre* (First published 1847)
Brontë, Charlotte, *Shirley* (First published 1849)
*Byron: Selected letters and journals,* (ed.) P. Gunn, (Penguin, 1984)
Ferrett, Mabel, *The Brontës in the Spen Valley* (Kirklees Cultural and Leisure Services, 1997)

**Everyday life of the period**
Laudermilk, S.H. and Hamlin, T.L., *The Regency Companion* (Garland Publishing, New York, 1989)

223

Murray, Venetia, *High Society: A social history of the Regency period* (Viking Penguin, 1998)

Pool, Daniel, *What Jane Austen knew and Charles Dickens ate* (Simon & Schuster, New York, 1994)


**Non-book resources**

*Yorkshire Folk-Talk*, by the Rev. M.C.F. Morris, B.C.L., M.A. (1892) transcribed for the Internet by Colin Hinson at <http://www.genuki.org.uk/big/eng/YKS/FoIkTalk/index.html>

Armley Mills, Leeds Industrial Museum, West Yorkshire.

*Life and Times Board of the Republic of Pemberley* at <http://www.pemberley.com> (concentrates on Jane Austen, but the archives are invaluable for details of everyday life in the period).

Oakwell Hall Country Park, Nutter Lane, Burstall, Batley, West Yorkshire (the original of Fieldhead).

The Red House, Oxford Road, Gomersal, West Yorkshire (built by relatives of Enoch Taylor, now a Brontë museum).

The Shears Inn, Hightown, near Heckmondwike, West Yorkshire (this former croppers' inn has a good collection of Luddite memorabilia).